MW01166588

BLOOD ISLAND

Blood Island

Allan Ede

I hope you enjoy reading my book!

Allan Ede

iUniverse, Inc.

New York Lincoln Shanghai

Blood Island

All Rights Reserved © 2003 by Allan F. Ede

No part of this book may be reproduced or transmitted in any form or by any means, graphic, electronic, or mechanical, including photocopying, recording, taping, or by any information storage retrieval system, without the written permission of the publisher.

iUniverse, Inc.

For information address:
iUniverse, Inc.
2021 Pine Lake Road, Suite 100
Lincoln, NE 68512
www.iuniverse.com

ISBN: 0-595-27158-8

Printed in the United States of America

I would like to dedicate this book to Laura (the first to read my book and wholeheartedly approve of it), John (my mentor), Kathy, his dear wife, and the Tuesday night Shredders (Barb, Brad, Chuck, Diane, Katie, Nancy, Pam, Paul, Rick, Rose, Sharon, and Suellen) who inspired me and encouraged me to become a better writer.

PROLOGUE

▼

The sound of Vietcong patrol boats droned in the distance, as oil-laden waves splashed against the bars of the bamboo tiger cage where Sergeant Spencer Hendran stood in chest high blackish water. Rigidly holding his arms at his sides, he seemed oblivious to the three Vietcong soldiers who jabbed at him with long pointed sticks. From the opening in the ceiling of the two-story prison, they laughed and cursed at him, hoping he would react to their taunting. Each time they prodded his bare shoulders and chest, infected with pussy boils, blood oozed from the punctures in his skin and mingled with the dark oily sediment on his body. But he didn't look up toward their jeering faces. Instead, his eyes focused on a spot in his watery cell where v-shaped ripples surged toward the bloated corpse of Dan McClain, one of his squad members. The man had died two days previously from battle wounds and malnutrition.

Now hordes of flies buzzed about his hideous puffed out face. Blood-filled leeches feasted on his entire upper torso that floated in the stagnant water, his legs dangling loosely beneath the surface.

Spencer lunged forward knocking his captors' sticks away with his left hand and grabbed the huge oil-drenched rat that had invaded his prison. Holding the vicious creature above water, he squeezed its neck with both hands till the rat—its eyes, bulging grotesquely from their sockets—quit clawing Spencer's bloodied wrists. Its long limp tail, which had been whipping frantically back and forth, dropped into the water. Satisfied the rat was dead, Spencer savagely bit into its side, and then ripping back its skin with his teeth, he scissored off a layer and spat it out. After completely skinning the rat and exposing the flesh covering its innards, he chewed on the meat, and with each bite, warm guts spilled into the water.

Spencer peered angrily over the rat's bony back toward his tormentors who continued to jeer him. He gnawed feverishly on the meat as if they would steal his dinner. "Bastards," he thought. They hadn't fed him in four days. But Spencer was determined to survive. No amount of anguish would deter him from his plans to escape.

Four weeks were too goddamned long to stay in this fuckin' place. He would make his break as soon as the monsoons kicked in. If only he had been on point that day, he might have spotted the ambush that had wiped out his entire squad and nearly killed him. A bullet had creased his skull, knocking him unconscious. Spencer knew that had been a lucky break because otherwise he would have kept fighting till he died. The battle had been savage. Bloody bodies everywhere. Men screaming in their death throes, some of them disemboweled. Spencer remembered that he had shot two Vietcong with his M-16 and had slit another's throat with his knife, the blood drenching his hands, but there was no way he could have killed the whole enemy platoon.

Why they kept him alive, he couldn't guess, unless they needed another pet to play with—to amuse themselves in this goddamned steamy jungle where everyone and everything rotted away in time. And they had other captives too. Some Americans, some South Vietnamese who were treated even worse than he was, and some highly trained South Korean soldiers who were among the best fighting men Spencer had ever been associated with in battle. Those guys didn't go down easy. He had seen five of their troops take out twelve Vietcong on a night patrol without firing a shot. In fact, they made no sound at all.

Using a mixture of their tae kwon do skills and sharp knives, they killed silently and efficiently.

Spencer had decided that he would make his break alone—fewer complications. But he would come back, and after freeing all the prisoners, he would blow this camp to hell. No, he would not forget those soldiers suffering in water-filled torture chambers where mosquitoes swarmed, unmercifully sucking their fill by day and night. The leeches fed till their bodies bloated with human blood and then fell, satiated, into the murky waters. Even the fuckin' rats and snakes preyed upon the helpless captives in their underwater cages. But they at least provided Spencer with enough food to keep his body strong. He would make it out of this hellhole and return stateside—and it wouldn't be in a body bag.

CHAPTER I

▼

JUNE 9, 1989
ELY, MINNESOTA

Spencer Hendran, clad in tight fitting Lee jeans and Polo shirt, opened at the neck, strolled leisurely toward the Last Chance Tavern—a popular saloon specializing in Black Label beer on tap, short orders, and plenty of conversation. His broad shoulders, held erect in military style, gave the impression of a self-confident man at peace with the rest of the world. He thought about his planned withdrawal into the Boundary Waters. It was not a vacation. It was a matter of survival. Provisions would last for a couple of months, depending upon how many fish he would catch. But he didn't worry about starving. He had learned by the age of ten how to live off the land; his foster-father had taught him well the ways of Indian lore, and the Green Berets had honed his survival skills to perfection.

After living in Ely for almost a week, staying with long-time family friends, Nancy and Burt Jaeger, he had decided it was high time that he venture into the wilderness—before he changed his mind or before he cracked up like some of his Vietnam buddies had done.

Spence was amazed by the increasing numbers of people flocking to the Boundary Waters. Fifteen years ago, only a few hardened adventurers sought solace here. Now all types of people were giving it a try. The young and old alike. Whole families. Some with children too young to walk. What the Christ was the matter with them? Didn't they know the dangers involved?

Oh, well, he pacified himself; he would outdistance these foolhardy ones after the first day. Most would call it quits after a day or two out. Portages would be nightmarish with little kids stumbling around trying to carry their fair share of equipment. Parents screaming orders, counting heads, generally adding to the confusion.

What Spence needed now was a little chow, a few beers, and a good night's sleep.

As he opened the door to the Last Chance, the raspy voice of Kenny Rogers, singing "The Gambler," rose above the din of conversation and drifted by to be swallowed up by the sounds of the night outside. The smell of hamburgers frying, mixed with the stench of cigarette smoke permeated the air. He sensed quickly that the dimly lighted barroom was over-crowded with locals and outsiders who had probably just come back from their sojourn in the Boundary Waters and those who had yet to earn their spurs.

Zigzagging through the mass of bodies, he managed to find elbow-room at the bar. The noise of the crowd was deafening. The whole place proved to be livelier than Spence could remember. Several young girls throwing darts shrieked an ear-spitting wail each time one of them scored big. Off in one corner, a raucous bunch cheered two burly men with their arms locked in arm wrestling. On the far side of the room, twenty or thirty people danced their hearts out, crooning along with country-rock tunes blaring from the stereo system. Waitresses, clad in white blouses and jeans, fought their way among the crowded tables, delivering hamburgers and pitchers of beer.

"What'll it be, Spence? The usual?" Ducky Dawson, one of the bartenders and half owner of the joint, didn't let patrons stay dry for very long.

"Yeah, and throw in a burger basket without coleslaw," Spence said, dropping a five spot on the bar. Ducky and Spence's foster-father had grown up together. He never tired of hearing their childhood stories.

Ducky should have retired years ago, but since his wife died, he needed something to fill in the void. Spence thought he looked as healthy and as stubborn as ever. His white goatee and thick head of silver-white hair, combed straight back gave him character of a dignified sort. Dark horn-rimmed bifocals added to his grumpy countenance. Spence chuckled softly, as Ducky, walking to the kitchen window to put in his order, stopped momentarily to chew out a couple of young bar hounds for some infraction of his rules. Sipping from the mug of beer that Ducky had clunked down before him, Spence continued to check the place out. Scanning the entire room, he noticed a lot of new faces. A healthy looking bunch of outdoors people with well-tanned bodies, many destined to be drunk on their asses before the night ended. His eyes backed up to a bevy of beauties sitting at a table on the far side of the room. Not because they weren't as deeply tanned as the rest, but because they were downright attractive. So vibrant. Laughing. Talking. Gesturing. Sipping beer and having a good time.

Spence tried not to stare, but he couldn't help himself. One of the girls struck him as being one of prettiest women he had seen anywhere, and he had been around—Japan, Germany, Vietnam, and almost all of the states. Shiny sable hair cascaded down to her mid back; piercing dark brown eyes and high cheekbones offset her finely chiseled profile and thick sensuous lips that puckered teasingly. Olive skin and a friendly smile, exposing dazzling white teeth that looked too even to be real, tended to make her especially alluring. This was a girl Spence would like to know.

Spence sized the girls up in a few seconds and then a few more; he was still observing them during his third beer. He hoped they didn't notice his stares.

His eyes were not the only ones focussing on their table. The boys along the bar were topping one another with what they'd do if they had any one of them in their pup tents. Spence resented their bawdy remarks, but at the same time felt a little guilty because he secretly fantasized the same things.

Lost in reverie, Spence barely recognized song after song blaring above shouts and clinking glasses and the occasional sound of bodies falling from chairs to the floor. Two drunks staggered by, dallying long enough to block his view, annoying him. On the dance floor, one man fell down and stayed for the count. His girl friend knelt down and shouted in his ear, "Get up on your fuckin' feet or I'm leaving."

Studying the four attractive girls, Spence finished his beer and fries. He washed the food down with a couple more beers while jabbering to Ducky about old times. Their conversation turned briefly to a familiar issue concerning the Boundary Waters. Most of the people in the area split 50-50 on whether or not the government ought to open up the wilderness to commercial enterprises and allow boats and motors in more of the lakes. The two of them agreed that the whole area should remain in its primitive state—no motors—only canoes allowed. Spence enjoyed the chitchat, but since he was setting out early in the morning, he had planned to make it a short night.

"See ya, when ya get back," Ducky said, as Spence picked up his change from the bar.

"Yeah, *when* I get back. Keep the beer cold, Ducky." Spence headed for the door.

Glancing one more time toward the girls he had been admiring, he was alerted by a disturbance at their table.

"Buzz off!" Spence heard the tall girl shout. Four rough looking strangers were harassing the girls.

"Ah, c'mon, Preshus. We're just funnin'," slurred a burly red-haired man with a scraggly beard.

"Yeah, well go *fun* somewhere else," the blonde cried.

"We're all friends here," one of the younger guys in the bunch chimed in. "We won't hurt ya. Just wanna talk a little, drink a little and…."

"And so you can have our table," the girl with the long black hair said. She struggled to slide her chair back, but a stocky, gruff looking man blocked it with his feet.

"Let me buy ya a beer, Pocahontas. Maybe that'll cool you down some," he sneered.

She glowered angrily and threw what was left of her beer in his face. His rage mounting, he wiped his face and groped for her as she slid out of her chair.

"You fuckin' bitch," he yelled.

"Okay, guys that's enough!" Spence said, as he moved swiftly toward them. The sound of glass breaking and chairs clattering on the wooden floor rose above the din of conversation as people cleared out of the area. Most wanted no part of the trouble, but several onlookers lingered, anticipating a fight, some with eager looks on their faces hoping for the worst.

"Lookit here," the big redhead snapped, "we got extra fun coming our way."

"Yeah, mister," the stocky man said, "do you realize you're fuckin' with four of the meanest, orneriest cats this ol' town has ever seen?"

"Just let the girls go, and there won't be any trouble," Spence said in a quiet, deliberate voice.

Ducky, aware of the rift, had slowly moved his sawed-off double-barreled persuader up within easy reach. One never knew what might happen in a barroom brawl. But, he said nothing, knowing Spence well enough not to interfere just yet.

"What'll ya do, if we don't?" a tall greasy-haired man said.

"Make ya wish ya had!" Spence snarled.

"Please, it's not worth fighting about. We'll just leave," the blonde said, grabbing her purse. She and the other three girls, catching Ducky's nod, hurried toward the bar. As the girls moved out of danger, Spence's pulse speeded up, and he prepared to defend himself.

"I'll just trim this nice guy's…." The big redhead had eased in closer to Spence, sliding a chair out of his way as he spoke, but never quite got all the words out. Spence deftly kicked him below his left ear and sent him crashing to the floor like a felled tree.

The crowd roared their approval and clapped excitedly. They were getting the action they had anticipated.

The greasy-haired stranger and the short, stocky man both charged Spence at the same time. He stiff-armed them under their chins, and their heads jerked backwards as they toppled over a table, crushing it and shattering a pitcher of beer and glasses. The young man just gawked. He glanced at the crowd. They jeered him, egging him on to do something. In the meantime, the big man had regained his feet. The whole left side of his face was swollen and was turning a brighter red than his beard. He lumbered awkwardly toward Spence mumbling, "You're gonna die, fucker!" He broke a beer mug on a table, so that only the handle and a jagged stump of glass remained.

"Hey, fight fair!" a man in the crowd yelled, keeping his distance.

"Yeah!" screamed a dozen others.

The bearded man flung a chair into their midst knocking several people down. The crowd surged forward in anger, but stopped when they eyed the sharp splintered glass in his hand. Paying them little heed, the enraged redhead stalked Spence once again. When he lunged forward, Spence, springing off his left foot, whirled in the air, and kicked him in his right kneecap. As the man's leg buckled, Spence punched him solidly in the nose. Blood splattering in all directions, he flopped over backwards, sliding on broken glass and spilled beer.

The youngest of the bunch jumped Spence from behind, clamping a chokehold on his neck. The other two rushed in for the kill, but Spence stopped one abruptly, kicking him in the groin. The man curled up in agony, moaning and cursing, and he finally collapsed to his knees, holding his hands between his legs. Then Spence elbowed the one on his back in the guts and flipped him over his right shoulder into the guy in front. The greasy-haired tough warded off the body flying at him and flicked open a switchblade. He lashed out at Spence, making several swipes with the knife. The crowd backed up a few feet at the sight of the blade. As Spence momentarily glanced in their direction, the knife-wielding assailant sliced forward, cutting his arm. Blood spurted out from the gash and covered his arm. He squeezed the wound to slow down the bleeding, then he jumped up, turning completely around in mid air, and kicked his attacker in the mouth. Some of the crowd winced at the crunching sound of the contact between Spence's foot and the man's teeth. He catapulted backward, cracking his head on the floor. Spitting out blood and fragments of teeth, he gasped and coughed, trying to keep from choking.

"That's all for that poor sucker," a tall thin man murmured.

"Jesus Christ!" a girl in front of him swore. Spence was only vaguely aware that the crowd rooted for him. Sweat pouring down his face and blood covering his entire arm, he stood waiting in a defensive stance. His adversaries, except for the one he had kicked in the teeth, slowly got up. Cursing, they stumbled weakly about trying to figure out what to do next, if anything. A spunky waitress stomped right up to the big man during the lull, declaring in a husky voice, "I think you bastards have had enough for one night."

The redhead responded by shoving a bloody hand in her face and pushing her out of his way. "I'll tell you when we've had enough, whore!"

But none of the brawlers made a move toward Spence. They just stood there, breathing heavily, their faces battered. Before they could get their second wind, Ducky appeared, holding his shotgun.

"I'll take over," he said, not taking his eyes off them.

Spence nodded approval, and pressing a wet towel that a barmaid had tossed to him to his wound, made his way through the maze of curious on-lookers to the front door. He could hear a police siren wailing outside the tavern.

CHAPTER 2

▼

Marna Wade shuffled along with her three friends down Ely's Main street. She felt thoroughly disgusted over what had happened in the tavern. She had been hassled before, but nothing like that. Why did those guys have to come on so strong? They were real creeps. She shuddered at the thought of their grubby appearance and vulgar behavior.

"You seem dazed, Marna," Julie Langston said, breaking her concentration. "Just forget those bastards. With any luck, we won't ever see them again. Hopefully the police will lock them up and throw the key away—at least keep them occupied till we get started into the Boundary Waters."

"Don't worry. I've wiped them from my memory bank," Marna lied. "But I wouldn't mind meeting that guy who came to our rescue. He was a hunk, don't you think?"

The other three girls nodded in agreement.

Sandi Moore, fearful of what might be following them, stole a quick glance back toward the tavern they had left in such a hurry. "Look," she said, her dark pony tail whipping the side of her face as she jerked her head back to her friends, "He's coming our way."

The girls turned in their tracks. It was *him* all right. His head held high, he strode in their direction about a block away. The four of them ran hurriedly toward him.

"Hold on, Sir Lancelot," Marna said, breathlessly. "We just want to thank you for what you did back there in the bar. Frankly, I'm surprised you're still on your feet." She smiled at her last remark.

"Wasn't any thing at all," Spence said, instinctively touching his arm. He had ditched the towel in a receptacle even though the gash still bled a little.

"I've been in tougher scrapes. Doesn't ever seem to be an end to guys who want to fight."

"Won't they follow you?" Sue Blackwell asked, a look of concern covering her face.

"Oh, they might want to, but knowing the sheriff like I do, he'll hold them overnight to sober them up and then turn them loose around noon. By then I'll be on my way to where that kind doesn't last long."

"And where is that?" Sue inquired.

"As deep into the Boundary Waters as a white man dare venture alone—almost to the Canadian border," Spence answered, rubbing a hand through his disheveled hair.

"And why would you want to do that? Are you purposely trying to lose yourself?" Sue hit a nerve.

"I've got my reasons." He looked deeply into her eyes.

"Well, can we buy you a beer or something?" Marna asked.

"What's the *or something* include?" Spence teased, but wished he hadn't because she blushed. "I'll tell you what," he quickly added. "Let me buy a case of beer and we'll go to where I'm rooming and talk for a while. How's that?"

The girls, after exchanging glances, shrugged an okay.

They walked two blocks to a supermarket where Spence bought a case of Miller-Lite, two bags of chips and onion dip.

Spence's friends were out for the evening, but he found the key in the usual place, concealed in a flowerpot hanging from the porch roof. He led the girls through the kitchen to the living room where he plunked the case of beer down on a long wooden coffee table.

Sandi, tucking her legs under her, snuggled into the corner of a soft couch. Julie sat comfortably next to her. Marna relaxed on the floor at the end of the coffee table, her chin resting on her buckled knees held tightly together. Sue nestled in next to her. Spence squatted at the other end of the table with his legs crossed under him.

He insisted that each girl introduce herself before he would give her a beer. They were only too happy to oblige. And when he popped a can of beer for himself, he said, "And I am Spence Hendran. Now tell me what brings four lovely ladies like you to the Wilderness Area?"

"Ah…Gee…Um!" They all began speaking at once. Finally, Marna asserted herself and answered his question. "Well, it all started two years ago when some friends of ours at college made the trip up here. They told so many exciting stories and showed such interesting slides that we got hooked on the idea. Since we couldn't make it last summer for various reasons, we planned for now. And so here we are, ready to move out tomorrow."

"Who outfitted you, or did you bring your own gear?" Spence stared directly into her dark, piercing eyes.

"A guy by the name of Matt Blake," Julie said.

Spence averted his eyes from her huge breasts with plenty of cleavage showing from her low cut blouse. "Oh, I know him well. He was a good friend of my dad's. You're in good hands with him. You won't be missing important equipment, if Matt packed your bags."

By 11:30, only six beers remained. Spence got to know the girls very well through their conversation. And he found himself telling them more about his life than he intended. It might have been the beer; it might have been the adrenaline boost he got in the brawl *or maybe it was because the girls were so charming and such good listeners.* Whatever the reasons, he had opened up to them. He had even told them how he became an orphan at the age of three when his parents died in a fire.

"Sometimes I dream about that yet," Spence said. "I remember Sheba, our big Labrador, dragging me along the floor through flames, the burning ceiling falling all around us. She managed to pull me to a window where a fireman grabbed me and yanked me to the outside air."

"My god," Sue exclaimed, shrugging her muscular swimmer's shoulders, "what a nightmare!"

"Did you grow up in an orphanage or what?" Julie pressed.

"Well, I lived in one till I was six, and then Dan and Sarah Hendran adopted me."

"What were they like as parents?" Sue asked.

They were really pumping him for details. Why were they so inquisitive? Why did they want to know so many details concerning his life? But somehow he didn't mind.

"Dan," Spence continued, "was a superb outdoorsman who knew the ways of the wild better than some of his Indian friends. By the time I was ten, he had taught me how to track a deer through forests where others would see no tracks. He showed me how to read tracks of any animal, knowing whether they were a few hours or a few days old. He grilled into me how to survive in the wilderness, how to hunt and fish and live off the land."

The girls eagerly listened to every little detail about his life, but they were especially interested in the last few years.

"So how did you wind up here with us?" Marna asked.

"My father helped me to become a pretty good athlete in high school, and my mother made sure I didn't slouch off on my studies. They were determined to make me a well-rounded student. Eventually, I attended St. Thomas College on an athletic scholarship and graduated with a major in English and a teaching certificate. After teaching one year, I found myself in Vietnam...."

"And after the war, you started teaching again right away?" Julie broke in.

She had just brushed over four years of hell in Vietnam with her question, and that was just as well. He had enough trouble trying to forget his nightmares without reliving them in conversation. "Well, first I took a year off, just trying to fit back into this lifestyle—to live again. Then I got a job coaching and teaching."

"Didn't you enjoy it, Spence, or what?" Marna questioned.

"I did at first. I liked working with kids. But that changed. Call it "burn out" or whatever. I continued to get disillusioned by our whole educational process. Too many students and teachers just putting in their time—getting through each day."

"What about coaching? Didn't you enjoy that?" Sandi inquired, a puzzled look on her face.

"I guess I got fed up with *both* about the same time. I wanted out, and I am now—for a while anyway."

He neglected to tell them how he had almost freaked out that last year of school. Would he have punched out some recalcitrant kid or maybe even worse—killed someone? He had come close. *Oh, so close!* While out jogging, he had stumbled onto a bunch of teenagers having a kegger. He spotted three of his starting-five players stoned out of their minds on beer and dope. He remembered how in a rage, he had torn off the spigot and kicked over the keg, sending it rolling on the ground, sputtering beer as it bounced through the crowd of teens. Some of the kids, not knowing who he was or not caring, jumped him, trying to knock him down. For a while, Spence found himself back in the jungles of Nam. Once again he became a killing machine, tearing into that crowd with kung fu. Those pathetic punks didn't realize what they had encountered—that this man-beast within their midst had killed more than thirty Vietcong regulars in hand-to-hand combat and dozens more in fire-fights. But it didn't take them long to scatter before he did permanent harm to their bodies.

The newspapers had, of course, made a big story out of the affair. Certain phrases stuck in his mind: "Teacher Brutality" and "Former Green Beret Runs Amok." Several parents had taken the matter to court, and in the meantime, those three players who had broken nearly all the training rules in the school handbook were allowed to play basketball until their case came up—and that would be after the season ended.

What a mockery of justice! It pained Spence to finish their schedule and not be biased against those bastards. Seeing their smug faces every day in practice made him sick. It took all of his will power to refrain from tying into them—breaking a few of their bones for starters. And it was that kind of thinking that made Spence fearful of what he might do to anyone else who antagonized him in the future.

Their record, despite the discord on the team, ended up 16-4 (including two tournament victories), finally losing to the state runner-up in overtime. All the fans were elated, and the school board responded favorably by offering him another contract with a substantial raise and fewer duties. But his heart was not in coaching anymore, even though he had compiled a 64-12 win-loss record since taking over as head coach four years ago. A lot of good, dedicated athletes deserved his time and expertise, but letting bad asses break rules and continue to play, soured him. *Did sports build character or just characters?* In some schools, if the players came to play reasonably sober, the coaches played them. Winning was the only game in town!

Spence didn't tell the girls about his nightmares either, how he constantly relived his Vietnam experiences, nor did he mention his hair-triggered temper that exploded with the smallest provocation.

"What are you gonna do, Spence?" Marna asked.

"As I said before, I guess I'll try to find myself in the wilderness. My friends from Nam call it, 'Going to the bush.'"

"Hey, it's getting late," Marna said. "Anyone for a last beer?"

"Not me," Spence said. "I've had enough for tonight."

"Me too," Sue said, as she stretched and yawned.

Spence stopped Marna at the door. "How about breakfast?" He was close enough to smell her perfume.

"Sure, why not." She studied his steel blue eyes. "You mean all of us, don't you?"

"Of course. Seven o'clock at Sally's Café," Spence said.

Spence wondered why he was getting further involved with them when he had vowed to get away from people—to be alone. But he didn't lose any sleep over it. They were easy to like—*especially that Marna*. And besides he would outdistance them in half a day's time. Not even charming women would keep him from his destination. There would always be women around when he got back—when he decided he was ready to live in society again. But a part of him wondered if there would be another like Marna.

CHAPTER 3

▼

Spence, wide-eyed at 5:00 a.m., swung out of bed. He never needed an alarm clock to tell him when to get up in the morning. He was glad that Marna and the other girls had agreed to have breakfast with him. He had plenty of time to perform his ritualistic limbering up exercises, something he had not failed to do for the last twenty years—even while in Nam, unless he had awakened to gunfire. After showering, a pleasure he savored for as long as he could, knowing it would be his last for sometime to come, he shaved, and wrote a farewell note to the Jaegers. Then, having put all of his camping gear on their front porch, he headed downtown.

Over breakfast, Spence got to know the girls even better than he had the night before. All except Marna. She remained attentive to the conversation, but she herself said very little, allowing her friends to rattle on about their lives at Briar Cliff College. Occasionally, Spence caught Marna staring at him. Wondering what she was thinking, he would give anything to read her mind. Her warm smile made him feel her thoughts toward him were favorable, but in what way he could not determine.

"Are you going anywhere near Lake Alice, Spence?" Julie asked, spreading jelly on her toast.

"Yeah, I could go that way," Spence said, anticipating her next question.

"Why don't you travel with us for at least part of the trip?"

"A good idea," Marna said, her eyes sparkling.

"Why not!" Spence agreed. "I'm really not in that big of a hurry to get where I'm going." *Why not, indeed. What better company could a guy ask for? How could he refuse?*

"Oh, you think we'll slow you down, do you?" Sue teased. "We've been practicing a little canoeing back in Iowa. I think we've got the hang of it."

"That's remains to be seen," Spence laughed. He wondered why he accepted their offer for companionship when all along he had planned to lone it. But then he glanced into Marna's dark eyes. Instantly, he knew why he decided to travel with them. That girl had some kind of hold on him that he couldn't quite understand. It was more than her beauty that beguiled him. He had dated plenty of pretty women. No. There was something else that made her excitingly different than the other females in his past. Maybe a couple of days together in the Boundary Waters would help him to identify the feelings that he had for her.

After eating, they drove back to Spence's room and picked up his equipment, then they continued north along Fernberg Road eighteen miles to Lake 1 which was their starting point. Their timing bordered on perfect because one of Matt Blake's workers was unloading their last pack from his van as they lurched to a halt along side of him.

"Hello," he cheerfully greeted them, his blue eyes flashing beneath the peak of a Minnesota Twins' baseball cap. "My name's Bob Conrad. You guys picked a swell day for departure. It's gonna hit 75 degrees today and no rain expected for at least a couple of days."

"Hi!" a chorus of greetings spilled out of the car.

"Where can we park this heap, Bob?" Marna asked, smiling.

"Right over there," he said, pointing to several parked cars. "Be sure to lock it and don't leave anything valuable behind 'less you want to get it ripped off. We've been having some trouble with that lately."

"Thanks for the advice," Marna said, wheeling their Impala wagon to the other side of the lot.

After returning to the water's edge, the girls stood looking out over the vastness of the Boundary Waters. Small islands, some verdant with wild flowers and heavily laden with pine trees, stretched to the far side of Lake 1. Intermingling with those were barren islands composed of huge, multi-colored boulders.

"Wow," Sandy exclaimed, "we're here at last. Just look at that primitive wilderness waiting to swallow us up."

"Well, I hope it doesn't digest us too," Julie quipped. "I would like to return to civilization someday."

Bob chuckled at their remarks. Pointing to a string of canoes on the beach, he said, "Yours are numbers 7 and 8." Then he turned to Spence. "Matt says to give you number 3 for as long as you want it. You can settle up when you get back." He had met Spence earlier in the week at their shop.

"Thanks, Bob. That'll do just fine. Want to come along with us?" Spence asked.

"Don't I wish I could, but Matt would fry me for breakfast. We're starting to get real busy. I'd best be getting back right now, or he'll think I fell in. Have a good time. See ya when ya get back." He hopped into the driver's seat and gunned the van toward the road, the empty canoe rack rattling as it trailed behind.

The girls waved at him till he rounded a bend in the road. When he was out of sight, they lugged their equipment to the canoes. They had six packs made of sturdy canvass. Two were filled with nylon tents, sleeping bags and foam-rubber mats; the other four contained food and cooking utensils. Marna started to set one of the bags in her canoe.

"Better make a quick check of your stuff," Spence said.

"Didn't you say that Matt was reliable?" Marna said.

"That's right. I did. But it's better to find out here if everything's in order rather than a day out."

No one argued with that kind of logic. After ten minutes of rooting around in their bags, they were satisfied that nothing important was missing.

Spence eyed Marna as she bent over her pack. *What a nice ass.* He looked away quickly, hoping none of the other girls noticed what he had been enjoying. He patiently helped them load their canoes, making sure that they were balanced properly. "Keep your life jackets within easy reach," he insisted. "Some of the larger lakes get pretty rough, especially if there's any wind at all."

After organizing their canoes to Spence's satisfaction, they pushed off with him in the lead.

*   *   *   *

The sun shining through the barred window of his cell caused Rafe Johnson to shield his eyes with his hands. He moaned and groaned for a while before fully awakening. Studying his surroundings, he saw his brother Joe on the bunk across from him. His two pals, Jake Green and Snake Franzen snored noisily in the cell next to them. Rubbing his hands through his blood-caked beard, he tried to remember why he had been put in jail and why his body ached so much. What the Christ! He was suffering from more than a hangover. What had happened to him last night?

*   *   *   *

Spence paddled for a few minutes and then let his canoe drift while he checked an oilskin map spread out before him.

"Lost already," Sue asked, as she steered her canoe along side Spence's. "Hold up a minute," she said to Sandi who had dipped her paddle for another stroke.

Marna and Julie pulled in close to the other side of Spence's canoe, back-paddling to keep from bumping into him.

"Nope! Just getting my bearings, and so should you. Take a look at your maps to orient yourselves. See where we *are?*"

"Not exactly," Sue said, shrugging her muscular shoulders.

"I think *I* know," Marna said, pointing with her index finger to a red dot on her map. Sandi and Julie both had grabbed the side of Spence's canoe so that all three crafts drifted along together.

"Yeah! That's it," Spence said. "Keep your finger right there." Then he turned to Sue. "Just a little more to your right," he said, as she slowly moved her finger along the islands on her map.

"Oh, now I see," she said, excitement in her voice.

"Good! Just hold those spots. We're gonna take a compass reading." He had instructed them to keep their compasses in sight at all times. "Now look ahead to Lake 2. Its entry is southeast of here. See? So that's the direction we want showing on our compass. Okay, take a look at those red dots. Each one represents a campsite. If we follow them accurately, we won't get lost. Every once in a while we'll take a reading just to make sure. Otherwise we could paddle around some of these islands for days—never getting anywhere because they all look alike. Have you noticed?"

"Yeah," Marna said, "they sure do."

"Okay, let's move out," Spence said.

"Aye! Aye! Captain!" Marna snapped a salute and spanked the water with her paddle, splashing him a little.

"Hey!" he laughed. "Good thing these maps are waterproof." Dipping his paddle, he made long smooth strokes. The girls followed suit, trying to keep up with him while squinting their eyes at the sparkling waters.

"Sue, can you reach my sunglasses?" Julie asked without looking back.

"Yeah. Good idea. Why fight the glare." She tossed the glasses onto a towel just behind Julie and then put on her own. "Ah, that's much better," she said. Looking over at Spence, she noticed that he was already wearing his, and so were the girls in the other canoe.

Sometimes they paddled for ten or fifteen minutes without anyone saying a word, just soaking in the beauty of the blue waters and never ending string of islands.

"Smell that fresh pine?" Spence said, looking at the forests that surrounded them.

"Are they all the same kind of trees?" Sandi asked.

"Well, many are in the same family, of course. But there are some differences. Take a look at those big ones on the right that tower over the others. They're white pine. Those scraggly looking ones are jack pine, and a way off there on the left are red pine."

"The white birch and aspen, salted in among them, give us a little variety, right?" Marna added.

"They sure do," Spence said. "Know your trees, do you?"

"My father used to point that stuff out when we went camping."

"Spence, is that a hawk circling above us there?" Sandi asked.

"Yep, he's looking for his dinner."

"Hey, look at the ducks up ahead," Julie interrupted, pausing from her paddling momentarily.

"I see them," Sue said, fluffing her dark ponytail.

"I don't see any ducks," Spence retorted.

"Just ahead of us," Sue said, pointing. "Right there. We're gonna bump into them if they don't move."

"Oh, you mean those loons," Spence said teasingly. "You're not the first to mistake them for ducks. Watch how they dive for fish. They don't seem to be bothered by people observing their eating habits; in fact, they show off."

"It's so peaceful," Julie whispered, as if she felt guilty about continuing the break in the silence. I hope it stays like this for the whole trip."

"Yeah, the Land of Sky-blue Waters. I almost expect the Hamm's Beer Bear to come tippy-toeing across the lake. Remember that old commercial?" Sue added.

"How come it isn't commercialized like every other tourist place in America?" Marna asked.

"Well, that's the big issue hereabouts," Spence said, easing up on his strokes to keep pace with the others abreast of him. "Some want the government to open it up—wide open. There's a lot of money to be made. Just think of it. McDonald's hamburger joints every other mile. Speedboats pulling water skiers all over the place, and all the rest that goes with so-called civilization these days. And some of us want to keep the wilderness protected in its natural state. Nothing but canoes and tents, no buildings and no motors and all that garbage; otherwise, these lakes would be simply crawling with people. Noise and pollution galore."

"Let's hope *that* never happens," Marna said.

"Yeah, let's hope," Spence agreed.

"Speaking of motorboats, don't I hear one in the distance?" Julie asked.

Spence cocked his ear to one side. "You're right. I hear it too. They're only allowed in Lake 1 and only a ten horse at that. When we get to Lake Alice, the only engine you'll hear will be an occasional jet, high in the sky." He wondered about that motor sound, but he didn't tell the girls. *Who could it be and is it legal?*

They arrived at their first portage, after two hours of steady paddling. It was just what Spence had guessed. Several canoeists were lined up in the water, waiting to land. The shore crawled with people. Several families were busy trying to ferry their stuff across the portage, and this was complicated by groups coming from the other direction. Several toddlers, carrying life jackets and plastic buckets filled with snacks, added to the confusion.

The girls thought it was an amusing sight. Spence, not overly touched by the scene, signaled the girls to paddle around the point where a small creek fed into the lake. He directed them up the stream about fifteen yards. There he knifed into the bank and stepped out into the water, pulling his canoe up on the narrow sandy shore.

"We can cross through here. It's a short cut," he said.

The girls looked hard into the sunlight to see a slightly traveled path cutting through the woods. They beached their canoes and tried to decide who would carry what. After some twisting, grunting, and gyrating, Marna managed to get a canoe on her shoulders the way Matt Blake had instructed them, and off she started, the canoe resting comfortably on her shoulders.

Sandi, the most petite of the girls, seemed to have the knack for shouldering her canoe. Once she settled it on her small frame, she traipsed off along the path humming merrily. The other two girls harnessed themselves to a pack each and trudged through the woods. Spence flipped his canoe to his shoulders and followed them. The portage was only a five-rod jaunt, so they all made it without resting along the way. At the half-way point, they met Marna who was already heading back to help carry the packs. The short cut had enabled them to escape the confusion of the other parties. Within twenty minutes, they were back on the water in Lake 2 paddling leisurely side by side along a corridor between two long island chains of reddish-tinted boulders.

"Spence, what do you do if you break your leg or something on the trail a couple of days out?" Julie asked.

"You send up a smoke signal, and a search plane comes and flies you to civilization, if the pilot sees your smoke, that is."

"You're kidding!"

"No, I'm not. Didn't Matt Blake explain that to you? Even if you had one of those new cell phones, they're out of range up here—for the time being anyway."

"Well, now that you mention it, he did say something about putting wet leaves on a big fire if we had any trouble we couldn't handle—but I thought he was trying to be funny."

"No one jokes about survival up this way," Spence assured her.

At high noon, they pulled into a small rocky, treeless island. They agreed to eat sandwiches only, and, after a little rest, push on with the intention of setting up camp early on their first day.

*   *   *   *

Deputy Hanks passed the tray of food through the slot in the middle of the cell door. He didn't like the looks of the drunks they had picked up the night before. They were more hardcore than the usual bunch they rounded up on weekends for disturbing the peace, and he would be happy when the sheriff turned them loose.

"What kind of slop are you serving us? And when do we get out of this two-bit jail? It's past noon already!" Rafe looked a mess. Both eyes were blackened in the fight, and bruises were showing on his cheekbones above his beard.

"Just take it easy. Sheriff Grabow should be back before one o'clock. I 'spect he'll have you pay the judge a fine and then send you on your way." He hoped that would keep them quiet.

*   *   *   *

By 4:30, the girls were anxious to call it quits for the day. Spence headed for a camping place that overlooked two lakes. They quickly set up their tents and started a fire.

"Imagine, steaks! That Matt sure knows how to please his customers," Sandi said, licking her lips.

"Enjoy them," Sue exclaimed, as she turned them in the frying pan. "'Cuz after tomorrow's hamburger for dinner, it's all freeze dried."

"Unless you catch some fish like this one," Spence said, coming up from the lake holding a sixteen-inch walleye.

"Wow, I didn't know you had a fishing pole," Marna said.

"I don't need one. The fish in these waters are so hungry, all you gotta have is a throw-line and a silver lure. They bite on anything that moves."

"We'll have fish for breakfast then?" Marna challenged him.

"No problem! You can help me catch some." He wanted to be alone with her, and that would be a good opportunity. He had enjoyed watching her every move as they paddled along during the day. He loved her smile, her gestures—everything about her. And that bothered the hell out of him. It wasn't the time for him to be getting attached to any female, no matter how good-looking she was. But he also knew he couldn't help his feelings.

After supper was over and the dishes had been washed and dried, the five of them sat looking over the lake that had nary a ripple in it. Mesmerized by the stillness and the beauty of the scene, no one spoke for a while.

"This is living," Julie sighed.

"It gets even better at Lake Alice," Spence said "You'll love the sandy beach, and the campsite itself is one of the best I've seen in the Boundary Waters. Actually there are several pretty good ones on the far side, and not many people paddle out that far. Most stick to popular spots, hoping to see black bears."

"Bears! I only want to see bears at the zoo in cages," Sue blurted, hunching her muscular shoulders.

"Chances are you won't see any," Spence said, if you tie your food up in a tree at night. Matt explained that to you, didn't he?"

"Yeah, he did say that was important," Sandy exclaimed.

"Speaking of that. No time like now to haul ours up. We don't want to lose our grub the first night out, do we?" Spence chuckled.

"Jesus!" Julie cried, as she jumped up and glanced toward the woods. "You don't think there are bears on this island, do you, Spence?"

"Naw, probably not. They usually favor the bigger islands. But we can't take any chances. Even raccoons will steal our food, if we let 'em."

The girls watched as he tossed a rope over a large branch of a pine tree that extended almost parallel to the ground about fifteen feet high. He tied the dangling end of the rope to the food packs and hoisted them to a position about ten feet off the ground. He anchored the other end to a birch tree.

"If you don't find a nice convenient branch like this, then you have to tie one of your ropes to two trees and pull your packs up over that. Make sure that you get them at least ten feet off the ground."

The girls were nodding in unison like they understood.

"Tomorrow night, I'll watch while you girls protect our food. Okay?"

"A good idea," Marna said.

As darkness moved in, they sat and talked around their campfire. Some of the girls were snuggling into sleeping bags wrapped around them. They had gotten sunburned more than they realized during the day, and now the chills were setting in. By 9:30, they were all ready for sleep, Spence included.

CHAPTER 4

▼

Spence lay in the darkness of his tent, listening to the night sounds, relishing the thought that he might have some alone time with Marna in the morning. But something about the stillness triggered the memory of one of his missions in Vietnam.

He and his two buddies, Digger and Cutsy, had been observing a small village for two days and nights without being detected. Their camouflaged jungle fatigues helped them to blend in with the tall weeds and bushes on the surrounding hillsides overlooking the tiny hamlet. The trees were not as thick as in the jungle valley below them, but the undergrowth concealed them well enough.

"Let's get the fuck back to camp," Digger whined. "There's nothing going on here."

"Yeah, guess you're right," Spence said quietly.

"Wait! Wait a fuckin' minute, guys!" Cutsy whispered. He had been peering through binoculars to the north of the village. "Jesus! Look what's coming to dinner."

Spence and digger froze. Scanning the terrain for movement of any kind, they spotted at least thirty Vietcong soldiers approaching the village clearing.

Their leader grabbed a young boy who was poking a stick in and out of a campfire, letting smoke trail off into the air. He shook him roughly, demanding to know where the village head lived. But already, an old man ambled in their direction. He smiled, bowed his head humbly, and welcomed the soldiers to his village, just as he would have welcomed Americans, South Vietnamese or even Montagnards. The Vietcong leader slapped the old man in the face and pulled the hair on his head, screaming for him to round up all of the villagers. Spence and his companions had crept close enough to the village to hear some of the conversation.

Within minutes, forty or fifty people huddled together in fear. The soldiers, completely surrounding them, were to be fed a warm meal and their packs filled with extra food for their march. All weapons and ammunition that the villagers might have were to be confiscated.

Spence and his buddies watched in silence as the terrified people scattered in all directions, obeying the soldiers' orders. For over an hour, the Vietcong ate their fill and rested. Some were not satisfied with food alone. Two of them grabbed young girls by their long black hair and ripped off their clothes. When the brother of one the girls heard their screams, he ran forward to their defense. A third soldier tripped him, sending him sprawling to the ground. No sooner did he get to a standing position, when the soldier smashed first the instep of one of his bare feet with his rifle butt and then the other.

Spence grimaced at the sight of the boy's bones being crushed. The boy toppled to the ground, sobbing, writhing in pain, unable to walk. The soldiers nearby laughed at his misery and then turned their attention to the naked girls struggling in the dirt with their rapists. Helpless, the victims clawed at their assailants, but to no avail. One soldier punched the girl squirming beneath him in her mouth. She spat out blood and teeth to keep from choking, as he mounted her. Holding her by her hair, he bit into her right breast and savagely took her. And when he was satisfied, he rolled off her, beckoning others to rape her too. Several stood in line, waiting their turn. One after another they pounced upon the poor wretched girl whose body, smeared with blood, semen, and dirt, remained still. Her agonizing screams pierced the jungle air, but she no longer fought back.

The other girl suffered much the same fate. Her first attacker had jammed the handle of his knife into her vagina. The second man took her from behind, smashing her face into the ground as he pumped wildly on her body. During all their torture, the village men, including, the father of one of the girls stood and watched in pitiful silence, helpless. The soldiers had picked the two prettiest girls, but the others, including the elderly, were never sure that they would not be sacrificed too. They had wisely hid themselves from the horrid scene.

The two young girls, practically torn to shreds, looking like rag dolls someone had discarded, lay in the dirt, bleeding, moaning, and pleading for help. But no one went to their aid. The leader of the soldiers who had witnessed the whole affair grunted his approval and finally ordered his troops to move out.

Spence had watched, biting his lip to keep from crying out in rage. He had wanted to run down that hill, firing his armalite and throwing grenades as he charged, but innocent villagers would have been killed in the crossfire. At one point in the torture, when the screams of the girls became maddening, Cutsy, his M-16 at the ready, ran toward the village. Spence cut him off and held him back saying, "Later! We can't take them now!"

But seeing that the Cong were disappearing into the jungle again, Spence wanted their blood.

"Are you guys with me?" he snarled, checking his weapon.

"You crazy, man? There are too many of 'em," Digger protested.

"How about you, Cutsy? Should we get those fuckers?"

"Yeah!" Cutsy said, rubbing his thumb across his sharp knife. "A guy can die here any minute of any day. Why prolong it?"

"Jesus! You fuckin' bastards are nuts," Digger wailed. But he reluctantly followed them down the hillside into the jungle.

They stalked their enemy at a safe distance during daylight hours, waiting for them to settle in for the night. After nightfall, they slithered in closer to the camp, but still kept far enough away so that they could slap at the mosquitoes and leeches that plagued their sweaty bodies.

The platoon, feeling safe with their numbers, had even lighted a fire to cook their food, and glowing embers still marked the center of their camp. After eating, they had passed around a few jugs of wine they had taken from the village. Several soldiers had come within ten feet of the Americans to urinate, unaware that death lurked in the nearby bushes.

By 11:30 p.m., two sentries had been posted and the rest turned in for the night. An hour later, Spence had stealthily crawled to within striking distance of the sentry nearest him. His knife drawn, he crept up to the drowsy sentinel. Cupping the man's mouth with his left hand, he sliced through throat and jugular vein with one swift motion of his knife. He pulled the man's face to his own body to stifle any gurgling sounds; the warm blood gushing from the dying man saturated Spence's clothing.

Cutsy had taken out the other guard in much the same fashion. Digger had slunk to his position for the attack. Moving in from three different directions, they lobbed two grenades apiece and then opened up, firing their weapons on full automatic, spraying soldiers who struggled to their feet. Only a few of the enemy managed to fire any rounds back and those only at shadows in the jungle. One man lived through the attack. Wounded in his right shoulder, he clawed with his left hand trying to raise his rifle. Spence, recognizing the trembling soldier as the first guy to rape one of the girls in the village, shot him in his left shoulder. The man spun around, dropping his weapon to the ground. Drawing his knife, Spence slowly but deliberately cut off his testicles and stuffed them into his mouth. The dying man, his eyes bulging in agony, tried to spit out what was choking him. His muffled screams got quieter and quieter, as Spence and his companions disappeared into the jungle.

CHAPTER 5

▼

Awakening after a restless night's sleep, Spence rolled over on his left side and looked out his tent window. Checking out their camp and finding everything in order, he scanned the lake front where he noticed Marna sitting on a boulder near the water's edge, her chin resting on her bent knees, her long, shiny black hair concealing most of her lithe body. She turned toward Spence as he stepped out into the morning light. They both waved without speaking, since it was only 5:30 and they didn't want to wake the others.

"*Good! She's alone,*" Spence thought, as he disappeared into the woods to relieve himself. Returning to his tent, he rooted around in his equipment pack till he found his fishing gear. He took out a long nylon cord with a silver lure and hook attached and then he pulled out a stringer.

He walked toward Marna. He was thrilled at the prospects of them being alone for a little while. The other girls were lovely companions, but sometimes their silly chatter drove him crazy. Marna mystified him to no end. Although she had been friendly like the others, she held in her emotions. He wanted to know what she was really thinking.

"Let's catch some fish," he said quietly.

"Where's your fishing rod?"

Ignoring her question, Spence led her down the shoreline to the place where Lake 1 and Lake 2 joined together in a channel about twenty yards across.

"Here," he said. "This is as good a spot as any."

"But what about a fishing pole?" Marna asked again.

"Just watch." Whirling his nylon cord above his head like a cowboy trying to lasso a steer, he flung the lure out ten feet from shore and let it drop into the water. When it sank out of sight, he hauled it in hand-over-hand. Luck was with him. An eighteen-inch walleye struck it immediately and headed for deep water. Spence let him take it for awhile and then jerked back on the line to set the hook.

"See. It's easy." He slowly pulled the flopping fish out of the water. "Want to try it?"

"Sure," Marna said excitedly.

After putting his fish on a stringer and tying it to a small sapling, Spence stood back and watched as Marna circled the throw line above her head, a smile of anticipation on her face. Her first toss barely hit the water because she held onto the line too long. Her second throw was better; it carried five feet out, but she didn't let it sink. As she pulled frantically, the lure skipped across the top of the water.

Spence chuckled. "The fish might be hungry, but they're not gonna work that hard for food. Throw it out farther and let it sink a little before you start to haul it in, okay?"

"Just wait, smarty." She whipped the line above her head once again, determined to do it right. "Watch this." She let it fly. Her lure hit the water eight feet out. Patiently letting it drop out of sight, she winked confidently at Spence. As she slowly retrieved her line, a walleye struck three feet from shore.

"Jerk it hard; set the hook," Spence yelled.

They had two fish for breakfast.

"It's about an inch shorter than mine, but I guess it's a keeper," Spence said.

"Whatdya mean?" Marna protested. "There's no way I'll let you throw my fish back. It's the biggest one I've ever caught in my life."

The other girls awoke to the sound of fish sizzling in the frying pan.

"Gee, Spence, you must've gotten up early to catch these," Julie said, as she sat down at the table.

"Hey, I'll have you know *I* caught one of these." Marna stood in a defiant pose, one hand on her hip.

"Didya really?" Sue asked. "It's good to know that we've got something to eat besides all that freeze-dried food."

"I think I can manage it again." Marna looked at Spence for a reaction.

"No doubt about it. She's a great fisherman or *fisherwoman* or just what does a guy call a girl who catches fish these days?"

The girls laughed at his remark.

"The coffee's hot!" Sandi announced. "Where's a hot pad?"

"Over in the pack." Marna pointed to the end of the table.

"Looks like another beautiful day coming up." Sue stretched her long arms toward the sky, revealing her strong swimmer's shoulders. "When will we reach Lake Alice, Spence?"

"If we don't get too sluggish with all this tasty chow, we should make Lake Alice by 3:00," he said, biting into a sweet roll.

*   *   *   *

Rafe stood off to the side of his tent, relieving himself. The sound of his buddies snoring amused him. They had really tied one on last night, happy to be out of that two-bit town and away from that smart ass sheriff. He didn't like leaving any place with his tail between his legs, but then maybe they were lucky at that. If the police had bothered to do any serious checking on their past record, they would have kept them in jail a lot longer. He had an assault charge pending in Iowa, and Snake was wanted for robbery. He rubbed his jaw, still sore from the beating he had taken from that son-of-a-bitch in the tavern. How he'd love another chance at that guy. And those girls! He'd do them up right too. Maybe they would get real lucky and bump into them again on their way to his Uncle Louie's place in Canada.

*   *   *   *

By 11:30, Spence directed the girls to a campsite on the northeast tip of Lake Insula. After a light lunch, they paddled down a narrow stream, the connecting link with Lake Alice that tunneled through overhanging birch trees. The girls chatted excitedly, knowing they were getting closer to their destination. They had met a young couple during one of their portages that morning who had been camping at Lake Alice.

"It was absolutely gorgeous. I wish we could have stayed longer," the girl had said.

"We were the only ones there," the guy added.

"Bet you had fun," Julie said.

The girl blushed noticeably. "Yeah, we sure did!"

*   *   *   *

At 2:30, Spence pointed ahead. "Lake Alice is right around the next bend."

"I hope so," Sandi whined. "My back's killing me."

"Mine too," Julie said. "And I feel so sticky. A nice shower would be just great, but I'll settle for a swim." The thought of their island paradise so close gave them strength to keep paddling.

And there it was! Lake Alice! The biggest lake they had seen so far on their trek. Green pines framed the wide expanse of blue water, and sandy beaches dotted the perimeter. Not another canoe or camper in sight. They couldn't believe their eyes.

Spence guided them straight across the lake to a large island on the far side. But, soon, he wished he had followed the shoreline. The wind grew stronger as they reached the middle. The canoes bucked wildly in the mounting waves, several times almost capsizing. The girls panicked. It was too late to strap on their life jackets, but Spence assured them that they would make it, if they paddled hard and headed directly into the waves. Enduring thirty-five minutes of steady paddling in treacherous waters, their canoes all but swamped, they made it to the island.

At the campsite Spence had selected, the girls all plopped exhausted onto the sand and giggled until Spence forced them into action.

"Okay, I know it feels good to hit land after that hellish crossing, but let's make camp and then we can relax. I don't like the looks of those clouds moving in."

After setting up their tents, the girls quickly put on their bathing suits and ambushed Spence, as he crawled out of his tent. They tugged and dragged him to the lake.

"You need a bath," Marna wailed, as they pulled him into the water and sudsed his hair with a bar of soap. They teased, taunted, and splashed him unmercifully, all of them aware of his slender, muscular body at some point in their frolicking.

Spence put up with their shenanigans for a while, and then he dived deep, staying under water for a long time. The girls worried about him till he circled around behind them and surfaced. Lifting Marna out of the water as he came up, he dunked her, as the others closed in on him. After roughhousing for twenty minutes, they settled down and traipsed in different directions, exploring their island retreat. It proved to be even more fascinating than they had imagined. Not that the trees were any different than those they had seen along the way, but the gently sloping beach, bordering the iron-tinted water impressed them. Multi-colored boulders dotted the entire length of the island.

The campsite's primitive table, hewn of sturdy logs, was a masterpiece in craftsmanship. The huge fireplace, composed of rocks and mortar with a strong grate over the top, would be convenient for cooking several items at once.

As the group spread out over the island, Marna and Spence walked together. If the other girls were envious, they didn't let it show.

*   *   *   *

The freeze-dried beef stroganoff for supper tasted better than they had expected. Sue and Julie took seconds.

"Wish I had a beer about now," Sandy moaned.

"Cut it out! Will ya!" Spence said. "You'll have beer at the end of the week in Ely, but, it'll be a long time before I indulge again."

Realizing that he would be leaving them in the morning, they suddenly felt uneasy.

"How are we going to make it back without you, Spence?" Sue asked.

"Don't worry. You can handle it," Spence said.

The impending storm failed to materialize, although considerable thunder boomed and lightening flashed over the lake, creating Nature's glorious fireworks.

Spence made a huge bonfire on the beach, and they lazed around it on their sleeping bags, snug in their sweat suits. Again Sandy teased, "Hand me another beer, will ya, Spence?"

Jumping up and running around the fire, he scooped her up in his arms and carried her to the water. "If you mention beer one more time, I'm gonna throw you into that cold, murky water. Understand?"

"Yes," she said, cuddling against his chest.

Putting her down, he swatted her rump as she scurried back to the warmth of the fire. They remained on the beach late, mesmerized by the glowing embers of the burning logs. Marna and Spence strolled for a long time along the water's edge, thrilled at the sight of shooting stars aiming at the moon. The slapping sound of dark waters against the boulders and the chirping of crickets blended harmoniously, creating a soothing effect on their spirits.

Julie suggested that all of them sleep out on the beach, but when Spence joked about them being able to see the animals coming out of the woods for a drink in the night, *including bears*, they thought maybe they would sleep in their tents. No one mentioned Spence's leaving them in the morning. They didn't want to face that yet.

When Spence entered his tent, Marna lay there naked, waiting for him.

"Marna?" he whispered, as he knelt down beside her.

"Yeah!"

The light of the fire flickered on the walls of the tent, as Spence reached for Marna's gleaming face. He kissed her moist lips and smoothed down her long, silky hair over her shoulders. He had dreamed of making love to her from the first moment he had seen her back in Ely. It was not only her physical beauty that enraptured him, but she also possessed a captivating, mysterious inner quality that he had not witnessed in any other woman. Just holding her took his breath away, as they exchanged kiss for kiss. Later, their bodies, rocking in a pulsating rhythm, exploded in fiery orgasm, their animal-like moans mingling with the night sounds of the forest.

CHAPTER 6

▼

The light of dawn slowly merged with night's darkness, eventually consuming it entirely. First, one bird, acting as a sentinel, hailed morning's entrance. Then another. Soon hundreds joined in the warbling symphony resounding throughout the forest, as if signaling the night animals to retreat to their lairs—Nature's day shift was taking over. Grotesque shadows and hazy silhouettes blossomed into trees, rocks, canoes, and tents. A bright red sun, glimmering off the tranquil waters of Lake Alice, rose higher above the horizon. Air, swishing through tall pine trees in the early morning breeze, seemed to be in rhythm with the sounds of water slapping against boulders along the shoreline. A hawk circled high in the sky over the island, ready to soar down and rake into its claws any unsuspecting lark. A woodpecker hammered a tree off in the distance.

But it was the constant chattering of a pesky Canadian Jaybird on a nearby aspen that awakened Spence. Feeling the warmth of the morning sun and smelling the fragrance of freshly bloomed flowers, he rolled over looking for Marna. Not finding her snuggling next to him, he remembered that she had slipped out in the wee hours of the morning and returned to her own tent. Such prudence, he thought.

He lay there thinking of the many women he had slept with in the past. None of them had stirred up feelings in him like Marna had. Her sensual ways of lovemaking radiated something special that he had not experienced with the others. Leaving civilization would not be so easy for him now.

Once or twice during his half-awake euphoria, he thought he had heard the distant putt-putt of a motor. But maybe he only imagined that. There were not supposed to be motors anywhere close to Lake Alice. It was forbidden by law.

After lazily pulling on his jeans and tying the laces on his Reeboks, Spence stepped out of his tent and walked slowly toward the fireplace. He smiled at the sight of Marna flipping a pan-sized flapjack. Julie had just moved the coffeepot off to one side of the grill. The aroma of strong coffee permeated the air as he approached them.

"Hungry?" Marna asked, a wisp of hair dangling over one eye.

"Yeah. For my favorite things," Spence said, remembering their night of lovemaking.

Blushing noticeably, Marna dished him up a pancake.

"The butter's right there. And there's some maple syrup in that packet, if you like," Julie said, pouring him a cup of steaming coffee.

"I'm not used to people cooking for me, but I think I could learn to like it." Spence grinned as he sipped from the mug.

"Then why are you going to—?" Marna stopped in mid sentence, knowing she had no right to pry into his personal life. His decision to retreat into the wilds had not been made in haste. She knew that. And why did she want to change his mind? Why did she care so much? Her body still tingled from their night together, but she barely knew him.

Sue and Sandy crawled out of their tent into the morning air, both of them rubbing their eyes as if shocked by the daylight.

"Hi," Spence yelled, interrupting Marna's thoughts.

"Lookit that blue sky," Sandi said, stretching her arms to the heavens.

"Another fantastic day in the Boundary Waters coming up," Sue added, after plunking herself down at the table across from Spence. "When are you moving out or have you changed your mind?" She looked toward Marna expecting to see hope in her eyes, but finding none, she glanced back at Spence.

"Oh, in a little while. Anxious to get rid of me?" he asked teasingly.

"No way." She reached over and touched his hand.

Spence's *little while* turned into the whole morning. After breakfast, he and Marna walked hand in hand around the entire island.

"I hope you find whatever it is that you're looking for. And when, and *if*, you decide to come back—well," Marna paused, "you know where to find me." She didn't want to push, but she let him know that she cared very much for him. And that part bothered her. She had dated other men but never felt the way she did about Spence. What kind of a strange hold did this older man have on her? She wanted to know him better. Much better.

"I've got to straighten out some things in my mind. Two or three nights every week I dream about Nam. I'm back in those goddamn jungles, the smell of death all around me, hearing my buddies crying out in pain. I don't know if I'll ever be free of the nightmares." He smoothed the hair down the back of her head. "A few of my buddies cracked up, even after they had been home from Nam for about eight years. Their lives seemed to be back to normal, and then the bottom fell out. One went crazy and started beating his wife and kids. He's still wearing a straight jacket for his every day suit of clothes, and another guy just packed up and left his family without saying a word. I don't even know where he is anymore." Spence stared out across the smooth waters of Lake Alice. "Last year at school, I—I about freaked-out. All I know is, I've got to be alone for a few weeks—maybe a lot longer. Right now I crave the solitude of the Boundary Waters."

"Just know that I'll be waiting to see you again," Marna whispered, drawing him toward her in a warm embrace.

"You're the only thing that's making it hard for me to leave." He held her tightly.

Later, after lunch, Spence set out across Lake Alice. Once he started paddling, he did not look back.

Clad in their swimming suits, the four girls lounged on two sleeping bags, watching Spence till he disappeared around a rocky island on the far side of the lake.

"He really got to you, didn't he?" Julie said, gently touching Marna's shoulder.

"Yeah, I guess he did. I feel like I've known him for a long time." Marna gazed into the distance.

"Well, it isn't like he's gone forever, and from what I've observed, he likes you more than a little. He'll look you up. You can count on it, Marna," Julie said reassuringly, her blonde hair glistening in the sun.

"I'll just bet he doesn't stay in the wilderness half as long as he planned to," Sue added, a gleam in her eyes.

"Yeah. Someday there'll be a knock on your door at school, and you'll say something dumb, thinking it's one of us. And there will be ol' Spence himself," Sandi chimed in.

"We'll just have to wait and see," Marna said, staring across the lake. She appreciated their attempt to cheer her up, but she was not so certain that she would ever see him again. And at the same time, she was almost afraid to think that her future happiness depended upon this man she barely knew.

"C'mon girls," Julie yelled, taking off her bikini. "Let's skinny-dip and then bake ourselves in this gorgeous sun." She ran naked toward the water, her huge breasts bouncing. "Who knows? It might rain every day from now on."

The other three wiggled out of their suits, and, after dashing wildly down the beach, plunged into the cool water.

Later, as they basked in the warm sun, their bodies glistening with oil, a plaintive cry of a loon echoed across the lake, breaking the silence, but not disturbing their tranquillity.

*   *   *   *

"Hey, it's my turn, Rafe. Give me the fuckin' binoculars," Joe demanded.

"Shut the fuck up, Joe, or I'll ram 'em up your ass," Rafe yelled without taking his eyes away from the girls. "You'll get 'em when I'm done." He rubbed his finger over his swollen black-and-blue lips.

"Why are we getting our jollies from way over here? Why don't we just go across this goddamn lake and fuck all that ripe pussy right on the beach?" Jake brushed his long greasy hair out of his eyes, as he flipped a switchblade at a birch tree ten feet away. The blade stuck the tree dead center with a *thunk*. He swaggered over to retrieve his prized possession without even looking at Rafe.

Rafe glared menacingly toward them. "How many times do I hafta tell you assholes, I'll decide when the real fun starts. I wanna make sure their hero is gone for good. Did yas forget what he did to yas back there, for Christ's sakes! Your faces look like they went through a meat grinder. Without him, those cunts are completely helpless, just waitin' to get fucked. I say we start across before sunup and jump 'em while they're still sleeping. That way we won't have to chase 'em all over that fuckin' island. Ya think they'd just sit there on the beach and wait for us to pull in? Do ya? Huh?"

The three men glared angrily toward Rafe, but no one spoke. They knew it would go his way. Just like always.

Feeling satisfied that none of them would dare mouth off anymore, Rafe looked through the binoculars again. It was only an accident that they had met with these girls a second time. On one of their portages, they had over-heard two guys ranting about "four beautiful chicks" they had passed the day before. "They were so goddamned sexy that we kept checking 'em out and missed our turn off. Had to double back. We lost an hour," the one man had said.

Rafe had pumped the man for details without arousing any suspicion.

"I think they were talking about going to Lake Alice," the other man had volunteered.

"Must be crazy," Rafe said, "camping out here in the wilds all alone."

"They weren't exactly alone. There's a dude traveling with them. He didn't say much. Just kind of stared through us like he was reading our thoughts," the first man said.

Neither of the strangers had asked why their faces looked so battered. And it was lucky for them they hadn't asked.

And now those whores were all alone. *All alone.* Rafe zeroed in on the raven-haired beauty once again. Brunettes had always held a special fascination for him. Even if they weren't that pretty or didn't have much in the brain department. As long as they were dark-haired and built, Rafe enjoyed to tumble with them. Most of the time, after getting them a little drunk, he forced himself upon them after slapping them around. But none ever had the courage to bring him to trial on a rape charge. *They didn't dare.*

It had been three whole weeks since he had a woman, and she was a prostitute. He had enjoyed beating the hell out of her, blackening both her eyes and smashing her lips till blood oozed out. The more she cried and fought, the more he pounded her face with his fists—*and the more aroused he became.* When he had finished molesting her, he refused to pay her. Cursing him between sobs, she had cowered on the blood-spattered bed, too afraid to do anything more.

Carefully scanning the naked, dark-haired bitch over on the sand, Rafe felt himself getting hard. He wasn't so sure that *he* could wait till morning.

*   *   *   *

Rounding the point of a large island, Spence recognized a familiar campsite, more primitive than some of the other camps and surrounded by huge boulders. Fond memories of fishing and swimming experiences with his father when Spence had been a teenager made him linger, just drifting. When the prow of his canoe touched the rocky shore, he couldn't help himself. He beached his canoe and looked over the island. Wandering through the woods, he came to the spot where as a youth he had broken a tent stake, trying to pound it through solid rock. He remembered his father's howling laughter at his antics. The sight of a huge boulder twenty feet from shore pleased him. He had dived from its top more times than he cared to count. He wondered if the fish were still as hungry as ever in what had been his father's favorite fishing hole.

Realizing that he had stayed longer than he had intended, he figured he might as well stay the night. After settling in, he did some fishing, but his heart was not in it. He spent more time just staring across the water toward his destination many miles by canoe and portage to the North. Knowing Marna, as he did, would make his journey more difficult. It was not long enough to call it love, but he definitely had deep feelings for her. She radiated special qualities that he hadn't noticed in other women. She affected him in a strange, mystifying way—a way that urged him to know her better—much better.

Spence endured a restless night in his tent, dozing off now and then, but awakening with a start each time. An hour before dawn, he thought he heard the sound of an engine again. It bothered him. Who could be this far out in the Boundary Waters with a motor? The average outdoorsman would not gamble with the law that way because the fines were too stiff. But when he sat up to listen more intently, the sound was gone.

At 5:00, he splashed cold water from the lake on his face. A heavy mist lurked just off shore. Not being hungry, he built a small fire to make coffee. After drinking two cups, he poured what little was left in the pot on the fire. He smothered the remaining flames with dirt, packed his gear and put it in his canoe.

Before pushing off, he thought he would take one last look at the girls' camp. He walked through the woods to a point around the bend and up a hill, giving him the vantage spot he needed—unless the fog was too heavy on Lake Alice.

Looking across the lake, he saw two dark shadows moving through the morning mist toward the girls' camp. Probably just fishermen heading for that deep hole near the island. But Spence's instincts reminded him of times in Nam when casual observations of what appeared to be normal scenes exploded into hellish nightmares. He ran to his canoe and flung one of his packs to the ground. Ripping it open, he grabbed his binoculars and hurried back to the other side of the island.

As the two canoes sliced in and out of misty pockets, Spence noticed that they were equipped with motors. So he had not been imagining their sound. Zeroing in on the occupants of the lead canoe, his eyes bulged in disbelief as he recognized the bearded redhead as one of the four guys who had hassled the girls in the Last Chance Saloon. He didn't waste time checking on the others; he knew they were the same four.

Running back to his canoe, he stripped to his swimming trunks and strapped a long, sharp knife to his waist. Holding his hunting rifle in one hand and his .45 automatic in the other, he studied the two for a moment. He wrapped the pistol in a watertight leather pouch and slung it over his shoulder. He put the rifle in his pack and hid it along with the rest of his equipment among some rocks.

Cool winds blew in across the lake making him shiver. A rage of anger engulfing him, his temples throbbed and his body stiffened as he tightly gripped the sides of the canoe to steady his nerves. How had those bastards ended up here? The devil himself must have pointed the way. Maybe they didn't even realize the girls were on that island. *They knew all right*. Besides what difference did it make. Those girls were in serious trouble.

Marna! Marna! Spence could see her lovely face. But then the memory of the sneering redhead blotted out the mental image of Marna. He would have to hurry.

Ominous rain clouds hanging low in the sky drifted in across the lake as Spence jumped into his canoe and frantically paddled straight north. Wind-tossed waves pounded the front of his canoe impeding his progress. He worried that he would be too late. His mind kept focusing on the dreaded horrors that the girls would have to endure *if he did not reach them in time*. His imagination did not paint a pretty scene. Rape was never pleasant. Never meant to be—always ugly, debasing, and painful by its very nature.

His mind flashed back to Vietnam—to one particular afternoon when the monsoons raged heavily. He had been on a recon mission with his squad. Returning to a so-called friendly hamlet where his platoon had been stationed for several days, Spence heard terrifying screams rising above the noise of the storm. Entering a small hut, he was shocked at the sight before him. A young Vietnamese girl writhed in agony, her hands and feet tied to stakes in the ground. Her face, a bloody, sweaty mess, she contorted nervously, her dark, watery eyes flashing from side to side. An American soldier, straddling her naked body, continually jabbed at her firm breasts with the lit end of a cigarette. He cursed and said he'd kill her if she didn't take him in her mouth.

Spence pushed his way through the soldiers who were cheering the tormentor and anxiously waiting their turn. When one of them defiantly blocked his path, he whipped out his .45 and shot him in the side. The man went down hard. Lunging at the torturer, Spence kicked him in the face, knocking him across the floor of the hut, unconscious.

For a split second, the victim's face transformed into Marna's, as an earsplitting clap of thunder cleared Spence's head. He had to reach the far side of the girls' island without being seen. He would have to slip by a few smaller islands and swing back south. When he got close enough to their island, he would have to swim mostly underwater across a narrow channel to avoid being spotted. Pausing for a minute to wipe his sweaty forehead on his arm, Spence knew that once again he was on the verge of becoming a *killing machine*. And that thought bothered him. What would he do when he met up with those animals? In Nam, that part was easy. "*Waste 'em.*" No questions asked. War made killing legal. In fact, body counts hastened one's prestige. And Spence had killed plenty. Not that he ever enjoyed it. The very first time he had killed an enemy soldier, he got sick to his stomach and vomited on one of his squad members. But usually, he had no choice. It was kill or be killed. And he was good at it. How many was it? He had lost count after forty. He had no idea how many hundreds he had killed.

A few drops of rain pinged on the flat metal prow of his canoe, bucking wildly in the rising waves. Spence's only consolation was that, if it rained hard enough, it would enable him to approach the island without being seen. Digging his paddle in deep, he pulled it back in a longer sweep.

Marna consumed his whole being. He had been worrying about all the girls, but Marna's image possessed him. If they harmed her in any way, he would take it out on their skulls. He would make them rue the day they had been born and definitely the day they made the mistake of hurting someone he cared about. *But would he kill them*? He would just have to wait and see.

CHAPTER 7

▼

"Cut the motors," Rafe growled, his voice all but muffled by a pocket of dense fog. The two canoes drifted silently for a few seconds in the middle of the lake—two eerie shadows floating in the morning mist. The four men, dipping their paddles, carved a path through the haze toward the girls' island.

After stroking steadily for twenty minutes, they spotted trees on the island looming ghost-like through the gray, soupy vapors. The first canoe bumped shore, making a slight grating sound as it knifed through sand and small pebbles. Jake jumped out and grabbed the metal prow of the canoe, hauling it and his companion, Snake, half way onto the beach.

When the second canoe pulled in, Rafe lumbered forward, and, after stepping on land, dragged the canoe so fast with a sweep of his right arm, that he almost tipped his brother Joe out the back end. Joe saved himself from a dunking by frantically grabbing both sides of the canoe. Miffed as he was, he said nothing.

"Remember," Rafe snarled quietly to the others, "the bitch with the long black hair belongs to me. The rest of you can fuck whichever ones ya want 'cept her."

Jake, standing on the shore, his stringy hair plastered to his head, rubbed his knife blade on his pant leg. "We're all gonna get us some first class pussy—one way or the other," he mumbled, glancing toward the tents barely visible in the fog.

Rafe leading, the men crept stealthily up the beach, almost going to all fours as the slope steepened. Carefully picking their way along the path, they silently approached the tents nestled among the trees.

At the first tent, Rafe, pausing long enough to squint through the corner of the window flap, grinned. The bitch lay sleeping, her long black hair cascading over the top of her sleeping bag. Turning to the others, he signaled them to begin their assault. The sun's rays tried to penetrate the morning fog as a slight cool breeze did its part to clear the air too.

Not saying a word, Rafe slowly unzipped the door to the tent. Accomplishing that without rousing the sleeping girls, he stepped through the opening, his brother close at his heels. Creeping on his hands and knees to Marna's sleeping bag, he scratched his whiskered face and thought how easy it would be this time. No danger that any-one would hear screams and spoil things. In a way, it took some of the excitement out of it—the nervous tension, wondering if he would be caught in the act.

Now, as he hovered over her, sweat dripping from his forehead, he felt absolute power over this sleeping beauty. He was her master, and he could make her do anything he wanted her to. *And she'd do plenty before he was through with her.* He longingly anticipated that first look of terror in her eyes—when she would realize that he was going to rape her. She'd pay for the beating he had taken back in Ely. *She'd pay over and over again.*

Marna had stirred a little at the sound of the tent zipper being pulled. Probably Julie going to the bathroom or something—maybe to start breakfast. She remained content in a drowsy reverie.

A heavy weight pressing on her body made her think that maybe Spence had returned. She dreamily pondered what pleasures that would bring. But she sensed discomfort—a feeling of confinement—unable to move her arms as if she were pinioned to the ground. She moaned sleepily, trying to free herself, to get more air—to breathe deeply—everything seemed so close. Twisting her head from side to side and licking her lips, she struggled to wrest herself from whatever it was holding her. She had to get out of her sleeping bag and inhale fresh air before she smothered.

Opening her eyes, she blinked several times, not believing the sight before her. A mammoth face, battered and bruised, clamped down on her mouth. She screamed, but only blubbering sounds came from her throat. He slobbered on her, biting her lips and tasting the blood as it oozed down her chin. She continued to shriek, but fear locked her screams inside her. Sour, fetid breath and body odors assailed her nostrils. She squirmed, trying to release her arms to fight him off, but to no avail. The weight of his huge body alone sapped her strength.

Raising his grotesque head from hers, he viciously slapped her face and then her breasts.

"Whatsa matter, Pocahontas," he said in a mocking tone, as if he were reading her thoughts, "no hero around to save you this time?" He emphasized each word with another crack to the side of her head.

Desperate and crying in terror, she succeeded in getting her arms out of her sleeping bag and pummeled his face, hurting him enough so that he put his hands to his head for protection.

"Fuckin' whore," he roared, an angry hatred blazing in his eyes, "now you're really gonna get it." He punched her in the stomach, knocking the wind out of her.

She writhed on her back, gasping for air, all her fight gone. Dizzy and nauseated, her whole body aching, she nearly fainted. Lying helpless, she could only watch as he unzipped her sleeping bag and ripped off her sweat clothes, exposing her firm breasts and the rest of her naked body.

"Now, bitch! I'm gonna fuck you till you can't walk," he growled, forcing her legs apart with his knee.

Her body limp, her eyes filled with tears, she watched, horrified, as he unbuckled his belt and pulled down his jeans. Even though weak and dazed, she was startled at the sight of his erection. Whimpering, she tried to raise her head, to get away, but he socked her in the jaw, smashing her back to the ground.

"Bet your hero friend doesn't have a wanger like mine, does he?" He slowly lowered to his knees. "You're gonna like this, bitch." Straddling her, he squeezed her breasts till she cried hysterically and tried to push him away, but it was a feeble effort. Knocking her hands down, he mounted her, savagely plunging deeper and deeper into her. Wincing and grinding her teeth in excruciating pain, Marna slipped into unconsciousness, oblivious to the agonizing screams of the other girls.

*   *   *   *

Spence surged ahead into the rolling waves, barely managing to keep his canoe upright. As the rain poured down in sheets, he tried to blot the notion out of his head that he was already too late to save the Marna and her friends.

CHAPTER 8

▼

Thunder rumbled more frequently and for longer periods of time. Lightening flashed from one cloud to another, and occasionally a jagged streak bolted from the sky and zigzagged down into the trees on the far side of the lake. Wind swooshed through the towering pine trees as they swayed frantically. But only a few big drops of rain actually fell to the table where the four men laughed heartily, passing around a fifth of whiskey.

"Better get them tents of ours set up before she blows wide open," Rafe barked after swigging from the bottle and passing it to his brother.

"Yeah, I spect all hell's gonna break loose right soon," Joe said. "But why do we need *our* tents? Those girls are gonna share theirs again. Right?"

"Sure thing, little brother, but I like a little more privacy when I'm fuckin' a bitch. Now you guys hop to it. I'm gonna get their packs down and see to it those whores rustle us up some breakfast." He walked over to where the food had been tied. The other three hurried down to unload their canoes, following Rafe's orders as usual.

*   *   *   *

Spence paddled toward the island in the distance with a vengeance. The rough water made it seem like he was moving backward two strokes for every one he took.

*   *   *   *

It had been thirty minutes since the girls had suffered the torments of rape. They huddled together in Marna's tent, sobbing and comforting each other—what little they could.

When Marna had regained consciousness, she heard Julie whimpering next to her. Before long, Sue and Sandi had dragged themselves into the tent to join them in their misery. Half-crazed, tears streaming down their battered faces, they embraced trying to draw strength from one another.

"It was awful," Sandi cried. "When he found out I was a virgin, he—he laughed and said terrible things to me and then he rammed his fingers inside me. It hurt so bad I passed out for a while. When I came to he was on top of me and—and…."

Marna hugged her, as she sobbed uncontrollably.

Sue grabbed a towel and spat into it. Not looking at the others, she said, "That weasel with the long hair forced me to take him in my mouth. He said he'd cut off one of my breasts if I didn't do what he wanted."

"They're all animals," Julie whined.

Marna looked helplessly at her friends. They held one another a long time for comfort—crying all the while.

"What are we gonna do?" Julie wailed, her blond hair dangling in her face.

"If I had a gun, I'd blow their balls off," Marna snarled.

"But we don't have a gun!" Sue's strong shoulders drooped. "Maybe we could make a run for it! Do you think?" Her moist eyes looked to Marna for hope.

"I don't know! I don't know!" Marna said, staring at the backside of the tent.

"Maybe they won't hurt us again," Sandi nervously stuttered, her body shivering like a frightened rabbit, as a cool breeze swept through the tent.

"Don't count on it. Those bastards are settling in for the duration," Marna said, peeking outside.

"Won't somebody from Ely come looking for us?" Julie asked, her face brightening.

"Not for two or three days," Marna replied, touching the swelling on her cheekbone. *And that could be an eternity*, she thought, looking at her helpless friends, their faces bruised. A lot could happen for the worse by then. Where is Spence? If only—if only what? There was no hope. They were on their own at the mercy of those beasts. Fighting them made them more brutal. Giving in to them sickened her. But satisfying their sadistic needs might keep the girls alive. Was it down to that? Just staying alive? Suppose the girls turned on their charm? Would it save them from death? It might work. It just might. But one thought kept hammering away at her brain. *Alive, the girls were witnesses. Dead, there would be no witnesses.* Marna shuddered at her logic. There was no way they would be allowed to leave that island. She felt it. She knew it. Even if the men themselves hadn't talked about it, they would not be allowed to testify. So it was escape! Try to find other campers who would help them or stay and suffer the consequences. And in the end fight those bastards to the death.

She needed more time to think before proposing a plan to the others. If she could keep them from becoming hysterical, they might have a chance.

"Come out of there, you fuckin' cunts. We're hungry and you're gonna cook us breakfast 'for that rain sets in." Rafe's voice reminded them who was in charge.

Julie clutched Marna, sobbing.

"It's okay!" Marna said harshly. "Let's cook the bastards their breakfast. Maybe they'll choke on it." She stepped outside the tent. Her hair blowing wild about her head, Marna stood facing the wind that had changed from short gusts to longer sweeps, gathering momentum across the wide expanse of the lake. Under other circumstances, she would have felt exhilaration, but now she watched in despair as foot high waves lapped savagely at the boulders on the edge of the beach.

Followed by the other girls, who walked as if they were in a trance, Marna approached Rafe, whose big hulking frame bent over the table as he unbuckled their food packs and spread the contents in little piles.

Veins of lightening streaked the sky, as eerie rain clouds surged in the direction of their camp. Sandi shrieked at the sound of a loud thunderclap, startling the other girls more than the storm itself.

Rafe jerked his head toward them. "Well! Well! Well! Here come our girls just as we remember you. Maybe even a little more desirable than before 'cuz we got yas broke in right. Hey, boys?"

"Yeah, only one fuckin' cherry in the whole bunch," Jake sneered, his stringy hair disheveled in the wind and his deep-set eyes blinking. "Imagine that! Only one fuckin' cherry. They've been putting out for lots of guys. Might as well get our share, huh?"

Rafe stretched out and grabbed Marna by her long black hair, painfully twisting it. "I guess you know now we want what's coming to us," he roared above the wind, "and *that*, Pocahontas, is *everything*. We'll go into details after breakfast. There's really no big rush, exceptin' to eat 'for it pours 'cuz we're all alone here. As I figure it, we got a few days to fool around—and that, Pussyhontas, could seem forever, huh?"

Marna, smelling his fetid-whiskey breath, grimaced as he shoved her toward the table.

"Now get your asses moving and rustle us up some pancakes and coffee. Time's awastin'. I can tell you want those tits sucked real soon!"

Joe and Snake struggled with a tent flapping wildly, trying to stake it down deep enough in the ground to withstand the increasingly powerful wind. The soil was gritty and very shallow; several times their stakes struck solid rock.

"The fuckin' stakes are too long for this stuff," Snake growled. "We're gonna have to tie the corners of the tents to trees or they'll never take this wind."

"Yeah, but let's hurry. I want some chow before it rains," Joe said, as he glanced toward the table where the girls reluctantly prepared breakfast.

Marna poured thick pancake mix into the skillet, oblivious to the sparks blowing wildly from the fire. The others busied themselves setting the table.

After anchoring the last corner of the second tent, Joe and Snake headed toward the others.

"Looks like you girls have been in quite a scrape," Joe said mockingly. "Fighting over us, I'll bet." He could see by their terrible scowls they were not the least bit amused by his sardonic wit.

Rafe and Snake wolfed down pan-sized cakes on their plates and slurped hot coffee, as if racing to beat the storm's impending downpour.

When all of the men had been served, and the food packs sealed shut, Marna and Julie sat limply, a defeated look in their eyes. Sue and Sandi stared nervously toward the lake.

"I don't think they like us much," Jake said, glancing at the girls who huddled together forlornly at the end of the table nearest the fire.

"Give 'em time," Rafe snorted. "We're just beginning to get acquainted. Right girls?" None of the girls even looked toward their captors.

If anyone had given any thought to washing dishes, it vanished when Rafe bellowed, "Christ! Here she comes!"

All faces turned toward the west and witnessed the torrential downpour that spread across the lake in their direction. A dark haze of falling rain blotted out the far shore.

"C'mon," Rafe yelled, pulling Marna from the table and shoving her toward his tent. "This time, slut, you come to *my* house."

CHAPTER 9

▼

The sky remained a dull, dark gray. Heavy rain pelted the metal prow of Spence's canoe. He floundered in rough water twenty yards from a small island, periodically illuminated by jagged lightening bolts. Paddling frantically, he reached the shore and pulled his canoe, half-filled with water, far enough on land so it wouldn't sink.

Shivering in the cold rain, he rubbed his upper arms vigorously trying to generate enough friction to warm himself. But, all the while, he kept on running through the woods as lightening flashed all around him, accompanied by deafening cracks of thunder.

He didn't know exactly what to expect on the girls' island, but what he imagined was not good. Too much time lapsed fighting the weather. But the storm would cover up any noise of his approach. And chances were that no one would be out prowling in the rain to see his arrival.

He sloshed through the weeds and undergrowth, doggedly making his way. Low hanging tree branches tore at him, scratching him and holding him back.

When he saw a clearing ahead, he crouched low, patting his holstered .45. He stood up behind a pine tree and looked out across a narrow channel. Nothing out of the ordinary. No movement of any kind except for the trees whipping to and fro in the wind. He paused long enough to catch his breath, then dashed to the water and plunged in, head first. The waters warming him momentarily, he swam to the opposite shore, staying almost completely submerged in the shallows. Seeing no one, he ran to the woods and dived into a thick patch of tall weeds. He lay there breathing heavily, letting the rain beat down on his outstretched body. His steel-blue eyes slowly scrutinized the area directly in front of him. Nothing but shrubs and trees, so he crept forward carefully at first, and then he ran, leaping and bounding over low-lying bushes. Spotting a man-made structure in the distance, he stopped. He recognized the open-air privy—a four-foot square wooden box with a hole in the top. He knew the tents would be ahead. He checked his knife and gun.

*   *   *   *

Rafe and Marna sat in his tent eyeing one another. After wiping his wet hair and face with a towel from her overnight bag, he lit up a joint and blew smoke in Marna's direction.

"Here, take a hit! It'll make you relax. Maybe you'll even enjoy being fucked this time." Marna reached for the cigarette and took a puff. She really didn't want to appease him, but maybe she could learn what their plans were concerning the girls.

The wind and rain played havoc with the tent, but the stakes held. The damp air was chilly, especially since they had both been soaked before they made it to cover.

"Where are you from?" Marna asked, feigning interest. She could tell the joint was working.

"Missouri. A little town called Camdenton. My old man owned a resort there," Rafe said, reaching for the reefer.

"Sounds nice! What made you leave?"

"Not enough excitement or pussy to keep two healthy bucks like me and Joe satisfied. We drifted around the country after he got out of high school. Went all over. Tijuana. Dallas. Mostly in the South. Worked odd jobs till we got the urge to move on."

"What brings you to the Boundary Waters?" Marna was getting more confident. He seemed to be opening up. At least when they were talking, he wasn't mauling her. But hearing sobs and cursing from one of the other tents, she knew the horror was starting again.

"Well, now!" Rafe said with a funny grin on his face. "What brings *us* to the Boundary Waters? Maybe the same things that brung *you* here. You know, canoeing in the Land of Sky Blue Waters. Fresh air, sunshine..." He paused, as he reached out and pulled her to him— "and fuckin'."

He kissed her hard on the mouth and squeezed her breasts. "C'mon, bitch. I'm getting horny again. We can bullshit later. Now get them clothes off or I' ll rip 'em off. I want to play with those luscious tits of yours." He snubbed out the roach on the sole of his shoe.

His abrupt change in behavior caught Marna off guard. She actually thought that she was succeeding in getting his attention on *other* things, at least for a while. Her mind whirled. She didn't want to be beaten again. But what could she do? She wondered if she dared make a break for it. Maybe she could lose him in the storm. But then what? How could she escape from that island? And even if she did, how could she find her way back to civilization without a map? *The map.* It was in her bag, the same one from which he had taken the towel. She glanced from his leering eyes toward her bag, just for an instant.

She removed her sweatshirt and leaned forward, pretending to drop it with her other things. But at the sight of her full breasts, Rafe lunged and nuzzled them, murmuring under his breath.

"Wait!" She said defiantly, pushing his head back. He stopped sucking her nipples momentarily and watched as she tried again to put her sweatshirt into her bag. As her hand plopped down, she grabbed her camera by the strap and swung with all her might, smashing it against his nose, knocking him backward, blood flooding over his lips and chin.

Before he could recover from the blow, Marna rooted for the map. Latching on to it, along with her sweatshirt, she sprang to her feet, still clutching the camera. She whacked him one more time on the side of his head, as he attempted to get up. He slumped down again, groaning and cursing, blood oozing through his fingers holding his face. Marna, clinging to the map and sweatshirt, dropped her camera outside the tent and ran for her life along the beach.

*   *   *   *

Spence crept through wet bushes and weeds till he got within twenty feet of the tents. He spread out on his stomach and looked for signs of movement. The storm was slowly abating. Rain continued to fall, but it turned from a heavy downpour to showers. Spence would have to make his move while the storm lasted.

Hearing screams from the tent nearest him, he bristled, rage boiling inside of him. Slithering up to the tent, he could make out the conversation coming from within.

"No! No! Don't hurt me anymore," a girl sobbed.

"Okay, then! You fuckin' whore, get over on your belly like I said."

Spence's razor-sharp knife hissed through the backside of the nylon tent. Stepping inside, just as Snake mounted Sandi from behind, Spence grabbed him by his hair and pulled his head back, making his throat taut. He savagely swiped his blade across Snake's Adam's apple. Snake's eyes bulged in their sockets, as he knew he was about to die. Gurgling sounds bubbled from the gash in his throat as warm blood gushed out splashing on Sandi's back. Spence jerked the man's body away from her. Whirling around, her eyes widened in disbelief when she saw Spence wiping his bloody knife on a rumpled pair of jeans. She gasped at the puddles of blood and the sight of Snake's head dangling from his neck, blood oozing out of the gash and the severed artery still twitching spasmodically.

Spence aborted her intended scream by clamping his hand over her mouth. "You're safe. I have to get the others." He slipped out through the opening he had made in the tent. Where was Marna? He wondered, as he slunk over to the next tent. Puncturing a small hole near the bottom, he peeked in. He could see Julie writhing on her back, a man on top of her grinding into her.

Spence crawled to the next tent and made another slit. The long-haired man was forcing Sue to take a hit on his reefer. Spence decided to let this man *too* live for a while yet.

Only one tent left. Approaching it cautiously, he ripped a hole in the back and charged through it. Bewildered when he found no one, he stared at the drops of blood glistening on the sleeping bag and the floor of the tent.

*   *   *   *

Marna raced desperately along the beach, her heart pounding, her full naked breasts bouncing from side to side. She shuddered in the chilling rain. Clutching the map and sweatshirt in her fist, she tried to gain as much distance as she could between herself and Rafe. She knew he would come raging after her and that he would brutalize her for what she had done to him. But she couldn't dwell on thoughts of being caught. She plodded through rain-soaked sand, afraid to look back for fear he was right behind her. However, before rounding a bend in the shoreline, she did glance over her shoulder, relieved not to find him following her. Maybe she would have time to slip on her sweatshirt and then hide in the woods. She knew she was too weak to swim through the choppy waves rolling across the lake.

She didn't see Rafe jump from out of the tree line. He hooked her around the neck with his left arm, stunning her, and knocking her backward into tall weeds. Dropping the towel that he had been holding to his bloody nose, he dove on top of her and punched her in the jaw.

"You're gonna wish you were dead when I get through with you, you fuckin' whore." Grabbing her rain-matted hair, he smashed his fist into her face. He squeezed her breasts and then slapped them repeatedly, as she cried out in pain. Straddling her, he bit deep into one of her breasts and spit blood and scraps of flesh into her face. He pulled down his jeans, and, after slicing her pants open, he savagely rammed his swollen penis into her. Marna saw the hatred in his eyes as she drifted into unconsciousness.

When he had satisfied himself, Rafe stood up, looking down at her naked bleeding body, the rain washing away the blood as fast as it appeared from the slash marks he had made. He kicked her in the side. "Get up, slut! We're goin' back to camp." When she didn't respond, he booted her again.

Her eyes opening, she mumbled.

"Telling me how much you liked that, huh, cunt? From now on, bitch, things are *only gonna get worse.*"

Unable to stand, Marna was only vaguely aware of him reaching down and pulling her by her hair to her feet. Her knees buckled, and she collapsed on the ground. Hauling her up by her arms, he threw her over his massive shoulder and trudged along the sodden beach toward the campsite.

*   *   *   *

Lunging out the open door of the empty tent, Spence stopped abruptly and pulled out his .45. He had seen Rafe coming up the muddy path from the beach, carrying Marna. Afraid of hitting her, Spence didn't shoot, but ran toward them instead. Rafe, alerted to Spence running down the trail, unceremoniously dumped Marna on the ground, and after pulling her to a sitting position, crouched behind her on his knees. He jerked her head back by her hair and pressed his huge hunting knife against her throat.

"Stand back, fucker, or I'll rip her wide open," he screamed.

Spence halted in his tracks. He was tempted to try shooting him before he could slit her throat, but it was too much of a gamble—Marna's life the stakes.

Marna stirred, opening her eyes, finally realizing the situation she was in.

"Spence," she moaned through swollen lips.

Spence, breathing deeply, his eyes wild, looked at Marna's bruised and bleeding body. "If you hurt her anymore, I'll kill you in a way you won't believe," he snarled at Rafe.

"The way I see it, *Spence*. That's your name, right? You don't have *any* say. Just drop your gun and knife and step back or I'll carve her from ear to ear." Rafe pressed the knife hard on Marna's neck; a thin crimson line formed from beneath the blade.

Spence hesitated. He didn't want to give up his weapons, but what choice did he have? He chided himself for getting caught in such a predicament. He should have been more careful. He had survived Nam by being extremely cautious. Now he feared the consequences of his carelessness.

Slowly drawing his knife, he tossed it, along with his .45, onto the ground and then stepped back a few paces.

"Okay! Flatten on the ground, face down," Rafe commanded. "Joe, get the fuck out here." The rain had dwindled to a sprinkle so his voice carried easily to the tents.

Joe, poking his head outside, didn't believe what he was seeing, but he carefully picked his way down the slippery path.

"Get his gun and his knife," Rafe barked, still pulling tightly on Marna's hair, the sharp blade at her blood-smeared throat.

But as Joe stepped around Spence, Spence tackled him hard, knocking the wind out of him as he hit the ground, face forward. Pouncing on his back like a jungle cat, Spence put a forearm to his neck. "Okay," he said, panting, "looks like a stalemate. I can snap this sucker's neck without even trying." He applied enough pressure so that Joe gasped for air. "You let her go and get in your canoes, and I'll set him free."

"Do it, Rafe!" Joe wheezed.

Marna tried to warn Spence, but Rafe had clamped a hand to her mouth muffling her words.

Spence, remembering the third man, turned his head to check him out. Before he could react, Jake crashed the butt of a revolver down on the base of his skull, knocking him out.

"'Bout time you showed up," Rafe said. "Must've been into some hot pussy. Maybe we ought to swap—this bitch is drying out on me. Where the fuck is Snake?"

"I don't know," Jake said, bending to pick up Spence's gun and knife. "Maybe he's sleeping."

"Give me that fucker's gun and then tie him to a tree," Rafe shouted. "Joe, get the rope out of our pack and hurry up!" Letting Marna loose, she fell to the ground in a heap.

*   *   *   *

Spence stirred a little, slowly regaining consciousness. His head felt as if it would explode. He realized his hands were tied behind a tree when he couldn't put them to his head to soothe the pain. The sun's rays, penetrating passing rain clouds, warmed his body, but he didn't get a chance to enjoy it.

"Mother fucker! You killed Snake. Now *you're* gonna die a slow, painful death!" Rafe bellowed, kicking Spence in the groin twice and then in his left side, cracking several ribs.

Reaching down and grabbing him by his ears, Rafe continued his harangue. "You're gonna beg me to kill you, but first you get to watch us *play with your girlfriends.*"

CHAPTER 10

▼

The noon sun shone high in the sky, its warming rays periodically blotted out by drifting fluffy white clouds. Spence eyed the three men, sitting at the table drinking whiskey out of tin cups. He could only hear bits and pieces of their conversation, but he knew they were discussing his fate, as well as, that of the girls. His head had cleared a little, enough so that he realized their danger. Despite the pain racking his entire body, he forced himself to think of escape. Sitting with his wrists tied tightly behind a tree, he breathed unevenly because of his cracked ribs. A dull throbbing pain in his groin made him sick to his stomach. Glancing toward the girls, tied naked to nearby trees, he felt even more helpless. Their sobs unnerved him. There seemed to be no way to escape, at least for the time being. But maybe their captors would get careless. He would just have to wait for his chance and be ready when it came—*if it came.*

*   *   *   *

"What are we gonna do, Rafe?" Joe whined, taking a drink from his cup, wiping the back of his hand across his mouth.

"I'll tell you what the fuck we're gonna do. If even one of those mothers lives to spill their guts, our asses have had it. Right now the law could get us for rape, kidnapping, and who knows what the fuck else. That's fifteen to twenty years *minimum* for me with my record. And I ain't goin' back to the pen. Not alive anyway."

"I'm with you, Rafe. Let's waste 'em and get the fuck into Canada to your uncle's place like we planned," Jake said, nodding his head.

"Hey, wait a minute, you guys. I don't mind fucking those girls, but killing 'em is something else. Count me out on that score." Joe's eyes flashed nervously back and forth between Rafe and Jake.

"Look," Rafe said. "You don't have much choice. For what we've done already, you'll be in the slammer for a helluva long time, and believe me it ain't much fun. A mean fucker like me can survive all the shit that goes on there, but a pretty boy like you wouldn't last a week. They'd rape ya, and I mean a real gang-bang the first night, till one of 'em picks you for their girlfriend or boyfriend or whatever the fuck you want to call it. And that's just for starters, boy! You want that, do you?"

"Hell no," Joe blurted, "but I ain't killing no women. And that's final."

"You won't have to," Jake said, rubbing his thumb along the cutting edge of his knife. "Me and Rafe will do that up right. Won't we, Rafe?"

"Yeah," Rafe said. He had been tossing cookie crumbs to a friendly ground squirrel that got within inches of his right foot. He flipped a longer chunk a little behind the creature, and, when it turned its head toward the bigger prize, Rafe stomped on him. It screamed a death cry as its sides burst open, bloody guts squirting out into the mud. "See! Killin's easy."

"Maybe for you," Joe mumbled, gulping down more whiskey.

"Hey, little brother, you can start loading our canoes. Take anything of theirs you think we might need. Camp on the other side of the lake tonight, and you won't even have to watch us."

"What are ya planning to do? Haven't ya had enough fun, for Christ's sake?"

"Listen, asshole," Rafe yelled, "and listen good." He grabbed Joe by his shoulders, shaking him roughly. "Nobody beats the shit out of me like that fucker did and gets away with it. Nobody! Do you hear me? And you saw what he did to Snake!"

"I hear you," Joe said, pulling himself loose from Rafe's grip. "But we're gonna get caught on this goddamn island."

"Well," Jake broke in "you just get your ass across the lake and wait for us. We got ourselves some unfinished business here. As long as we got to waste 'em, we might as well have some fun doing it, being the penalty is just the same. But you damn well better be there when we come for you. The graveyards are full of guys who fucked their friends and relatives."

"He's right, Joe. But I know we don't have to worry about you. You're not stupid." Rafe looked at his brother for some kind of agreement, but Joe only glared at him without saying a word.

"Time's a wastin', Rafe, we'd better get on with it. We gotta bury poor ol' Snake 'for those fucking flies carry him off," Jake said.

"Let's kill this bottle first. It's gonna be a long day." Rafe filled his cup and passed the fifth to Joe who hesitated but then poured himself a round.

*   *   *   *

Spence watched as Rafe and Jake dragged Snake's body behind two ropes tied around his upper arms. The nearly severed head with eyes still bulging wide open bounced hideously along the ground, catching now and then on snags. It would take them quite a while to find soil deep enough to bury a body. That would buy him a little time. He checked to make sure Joe was still down by the lake, loading their canoes.

"Marna," he whispered, "can you hear me?"

Marna sat on the ground tied to a tree about ten feet away from Spence. Her chin hung down on her chest, her eyes closed. Upon hearing his voice, she made an effort to raise her head. "I'm sorry you came back, Spence, even though I prayed that you would," she mumbled, her words broken and slow in coming.

"Don't be sorry. I'm the one who's sorry, letting those bastards get the drop on me. Can you loosen your ropes at all? That goes for all of you girls. Wriggle your wrists hard, even if it hurts. My ropes are too tight. They won't give any."

"Spence," Sandi cried, "what are they gonna do to us? Will they let us go?"

"I don't know. What about your ropes?" He knew their fate *only too well*. But what good would it do to tell them.

"Mine won't budge," Julie said.

"Mine neither," Sue added.

"Shhhhh! That other guy is coming back," Spence warned them. He studied the man's eyes as he walked toward the two remaining tents. He didn't seem as hardcore as the other two. His heart was not in murder. "Hey, you," Spence called out to him.

Joe turned toward him. "Whatdya want?"

"Untie us and let us go before those other guys get back."

"Just like that, huh. *Untie you*," he mocked. "Why should I?"

"Because you'll be in jail a long time if you don't. I overheard what that big guy was telling you about prison, and he's right. *You* don't want to go there."

"You only go to the pen if you get caught. There's no turning back. What's done is done."

"Please help us." Sandi pleaded. "You're our only hope. My father's got a lot of money. He'd make it worth your while. Just let us go."

"Jesus, don't you understand. Money won't keep me out of jail, if we're caught. And besides, do you think I'd fuck my own brother?"

"*Your brother*," Spence said in disgust. "Do you think he cares about you? Why would he get you into such a mess if he does?"

"You shut up about Rafe, do you hear," Joe screamed, kicking Spence hard on his hip. "You don't know nothing about us."

Spence growled in obvious pain, "If the law doesn't catch up with you, I've got some Vietnam buddies who'll track you to Hell and back. You won't ever be able to sleep nights for fear they're on to you. And when they do get you, you'll wish you had never been born."

"Fuck this shit," Joe said as he stormed off toward the tents.

Well, it was with a try. Spence gave him something to think about anyway. Maybe it would sink in later. And just *maybe*, he would help them. But he knew he was grabbing at straws. The guy seemed to have a bond with his brother. Call it love—better love, hate, and fear all mixed together. But there was *something* between them all right.

"Are they gonna kill us, Spence?" Sandi asked, tears flooding her eyes and running down her cheeks. Are they? Tell me!"

"How does he know any more than we do?" Marna said, her voice faltering. "We know what bastards they are. Expect the worst. Just pray they make it quick."

"Oh, my god," Julie wailed. "Won't somebody come looking for us?"

"Not till dark tomorrow night," Sue answered in between sobs.

Spence guessed that all the girls now realized that they would be murdered. He was relieved he didn't have to tell them what he and, he suspected, Marna knew all along. Not that it made much difference. They would find out soon enough what was in store for them.

*   *   *   *

Rafe and Jake, their faces sweaty, lumbered out of the woods carrying camp shovels. When they got to the spot where their captives were tied, they stopped.

"Still here, whores? And your boyfriend too? Well, that's good 'cuz we told Snake—he was a good ol' boy you know—we told him we'd have a party in his honor," Rafe sneered. Walking over to Spence, he put the blade of the shovel to his throat. "It would be easy to chop your head off right now, but then you'd miss the party, and *you* are a special guest.

Spence, the sharp metal pressing against his Adam's apple, wanted to kick him in the groin. But it would mean his death then and there. Better to wait. They might get careless yet.

"Let's see your brother off and then get on with our little party," Jake said.

They continued on down the path to the beach where Joe sat next to the canoes on a boulder, swigging from a bottle of whiskey. After talking for a few minutes, Rafe and Jake glanced toward Spence. He must have told them about their conversation. Not that it mattered, except that it was probably unlikely that Joe would help them now.

Spence turned to the girls. It sickened him to see them suffer, yet he envisioned that their situation would be unbearable before long. *If only he had not failed.* He had been out of training for too many years, the kind of training that would have sharpened his instincts. He should have killed all three of them when they were occupied with the girls in the tents. And then he should have stalked more carefully the last man who had Marna. But it was his special feelings for her that made him want to free her first. He didn't deny that. He tried telling himself that was a natural reaction. But the fact remained—*he had blown* it. Now all of them were tied like animals waiting to be slaughtered. He had lived on the brink of death many times in Vietnam, but never had he given up hope like he found himself doing now. He wished he had the right words to say to the girls to prepare them for their inevitable butchering, *but he didn't.*

Rafe chopped holes in the girls' canoes, and the three men filled them with large rocks. Jake and Rafe watched, as Joe pulled them behind his motored-canoe out to deep water where he cut them loose, and stayed to make sure they sank to the bottom. He then continued across the calm lake, sunlight and clouds reflecting off the water.

Jake lifted a two-gallon can of gasoline out of the remaining canoe, and then the two men tromped up the path toward their captives, both clutching bottles of whiskey.

"They're still here," Rafe said mockingly, "I would have left if I was you. But I'm glad you didn't 'cuz now we can have our party. Hey, soldier boy, now I know where you learned to fight so good. Ya whupped four of us. But then ya didn't fight fair 'cuz ya used your feet, like this." He booted Spence on the left side of his face, cracking his cheekbone. "See how it feels, tough guy."

*   *   *   *

When Spence returned to consciousness, it felt as if someone had smashed all the bones in his head with a sledgehammer. But pain meant he was still alive. He forced his eyes open. He winced at the grisly scene before him. Marna, her body bruised and still bleeding in places, was spread-eagled on a sleeping bag on the ground. Rafe sat next to her, his bearded face sweaty, his red hair hanging down in his bloodshot eyes. He took a gulp of whiskey, staring at Spence all the while. "Glad you're awake. I thought we might have to go on without you. Jake, c'mere and tell our tin soldier what we planned while he was taking a nap."

Spence slowly moved his aching head toward Jake. Sandi hung by a rope, her hands over her head, her feet barely touching the ground. The rope had been slung over a tree limb, the other end anchored to the tree trunk. She whimpered, twisting around and around, trying to get loose. Jake swatted her bare rump before walking, whiskey bottle in hand, closer to Spence.

Taking a drink, he stood facing him, his long stringy hair, dangling over his pockmarked face. "We've decided to make ourselves a movie. All the girls agreed to help, and I'm sure you will too. Even the weather is cooperating. Now, we got every thing we need right here on this island. We got a director and producer, a scriptwriter—actually we'll make it up as we go along. We got actresses and actors. The only thing we don't have is a movie camera, and that's a shame 'cuz movies like this are becoming very popular. Saw one when I was in L.A. a couple of years ago; it really turned me on. And I'm sure this one will turn all of us on, including you, hero. Now you just sit there in your same seat and be a good spectator for the time bein'. Did I leave anything out, Rafe?"

"Yeah, the title," Rafe laughed. "Tell him the title."

"Gees, yeah, I plum forgot. We're gonna call it *Snuff*. Haw! Haw! Do you like that, soldier boy?"

"You dirty, miserable cocksuckers! You'd better make goddamn sure I'm dead when you leave here. And that'll only save your cowardly weasel asses for a little while till my buddies hunt you down." Spence had trouble spitting the words out, but they heard him all right.

"Shut the fuck up," Rafe fumed. "*You and your fuckin' Green Beret friends and what they're gonna do to us*! We live for *now*. And *now* is *our* time."

"Let's gag that mother fucker," Jake screamed, heading for the tent. Returning quickly with a strip of cloth from a sweatshirt, he put a knot in the middle and brusquely tied it over Spence's mouth.

As he was being gagged, Spence realized that Rafe had wandered within striking distance. He launched a kick to his groin, hoping he would bend forward so he could deal a deathblow to his throat. But the impact knocked him backwards holding his crotch. He writhed on the ground out of reach, cursing and bellowing in agony.

Jake jumped from behind the tree with his knife drawn. "I'm gonna waste this fucker now," he growled.

"No! No! *He's mine*," Rafe coughed, as he got to his feet. "Hold that blade to his fuckin' throat for a minute." Staggering over to Spence, he kicked him in the ribs. Spence, vaguely aware of Marna's screaming, passed out again.

Upon awakening, Spence, even though his entire body throbbed in excruciating pain, noticed several changes in the *live movie*. He was completely naked; his legs were spread apart and tied to stakes in the ground. A small fire burned near where Sandi hung by a rope. Rafe stood naked leering down at Marna.

"Since this is strictly a porn movie, we're all gonna be buck-naked. Besides, soldier, I want to see your cock salute when I go around-the-world with your girlfriend here. But first I want her undivided attention." He walked over to the fire and picked out a sick, its tip red-hot. Approaching Marna, he knelt down beside her. Grabbing one of her breasts, he burnt the exposed flesh where he had bitten her. She shrieked and squirmed, her head twisting from side to side.

"Now, bitch, listen good. You're gonna give me a *super* blow-job for the benefit of your friend here. See if he enjoys it as much as *we* do." He straddled her, sitting on her breasts, his knees resting on the ground. Grabbing her by the hair, he pulled her head up slightly, his penis pushing on her lips. "Now take me nice and slow, baby, lots of sucking action and no teeth, or *it's back to the coals again.*"

Spence strained against his bonds, animal-like sounds coming through his gag. Jake stood nearby, a nasty smile on his face. The other three girls, including Sandi, watched in horror. They screamed and cursed in a frenzy. Sue was the most vociferous of the group. "You, fucking psycho bastards, let her alone!" her voice rising above the others. "They're gonna lock you animals up in cages where you belong."

Jake's smirk turned to anger. He ran swiftly over to Sue. "This oughtta shut you up, whore." He pulled out his knife and stabbed her in the throat, pinning her to the tree. Her tongue lapping, her eyes popping out of their sockets, her head jerking back and forth spasmodically. Blood gushed out, spraying Jake's legs from his kneecaps on down—a bright red.

Julie and Sandi screamed hysterically, their mouths wide open, vocal cords taut, their tongues hanging out.

"Jesus Christ," Jake yelled. "Shut uuuuuppp!" He ran wildly to the tent, and after returning with pieces of sweatshirts, he grabbed Sandi by her hair. Slapping her twice in the face, he stuffed bits of cloth in her mouth and gagged her, leaving her dance frenziedly on tiptoe. Hurrying over to Julie who continued to wail uncontrollably, he backhanded her across her jaw before gagging her too.

Rafe remained on top of Marna, his limp penis, dripping semen on her lips. She coughed and spit, desperately trying to rid herself of his sperm. "You're supposed to keep it down," Rafe scowled, "just like medicine." He pinched her lips shut, forcing her to swallow. "What was all that screaming?" he asked, realizing that Jake stood next to him.

"We got one actress less," Jake said, rubbing the blood from his legs with a towel. "But that's okay. I *really* didn't have a big part for her anyway. And since we're making a budget flick, it's just as well. It'll speed things up. Hey, Rafe, did she give ya good head?"

"Not bad at all, considerin'. The best part was watching *his* eyes as I pumped away in her throat. I think he got his rocks off too." They both laughed.

Spence's eyes glared through them, his mind suspended in space and time. He had never before willed his own death, *but now he wanted to die.*

"I finally got those whores to quiet down while you were gagging this bitch the way all cunts oughtta be gagged—with pumped up cock. Do you think anybody heard their screams?"

"I hope not, but it might not hurt to take a look on the backside of the island," Rafe said, flapping his penis a few times in Marna's face before standing up.

"You gonna put your clothes on, Rafe?"

"Naw, I'm getting to like being naked, especially since that sun is so warm and there's hardly any breeze at all. I think I'll strap on a gun though, just in case."

"Stay on the set everyone. The cameras for our "Chick Flick"—or maybe we'd better call it a "Dick Flick"—will be rolling in short order," Jake smirked. Passing by Sandi, he pinched one of her breasts. "*And you, pretty-miss-rich-bitch*, get to share the spotlight when I come back to get *my* jollies."

Sandi dangled, straining on her ropes, her eyes flashing wildly.

Rafe paused a few seconds to check out Sue's corpse. Hordes of flies already congregated on her bloody body, and a thin trickle of ants had reached her stomach. "Jesus, I guess she did buy the farm. What a pity! Such nice tits going to waste. But I'd say we still have plenty to go around, hey, Jake?"

"Yeah, I got a hard on already. Let's hustle so *it* doesn't go to waste too."

The two men disappeared into the woods. Only the hum of buzzing flies indicated any life at the grotesque scene they left behind.

CHAPTER 11

▼

Trying to block out the girls' torture from his mind, Spence drifted into a deep, dark void to a time when he had been captured in Vietnam. *Engulfed in total blackness, he could hear Huey choppers whirling above him, and, from other sounds he could tell that Puff-the-Magic-Dragon was sweeping in low, her devastating machine guns spraying death throughout the village. They had been on a hit-and-run mission in enemy territory. Intelligence had confirmed that the villagers were Vietcong regulars in disguise who had wiped out an American platoon three days before.*

When the Phantom jets had disappeared, after making a napalm strike, the surviving Cong had scattered in all directions. Spence, undercover with his squad in the bush, observed a man who didn't seem to be running as fast as the rest of the fleeing soldiers. He continually checked over his shoulder to see if he was being followed. Spence stalked him out of curiosity. The man, assuming that he would not be seen, reached down and grabbed a bush, pulling it upward, revealing a trapdoor that raised, as if on springs, with the shrub. His careful entry into the opening convinced Spence that it was booby-trapped. After waiting several minutes, Spence followed him into what turned out to be a tunnel. Carefully bypassing a neatly concealed trip-wire that would have blown any unsuspecting soul to smithereens,

Spence closed the door and remained motionless on his belly, orienting himself to the darkness.

He lay there for a long time, listening intently for sounds other than the war raging above him. He remembered hearing about such secret tunnels that seemingly swallowed up whole armies, but he had never talked to anyone who had actually seen one. He did know that a special unit had been trained to seek out and destroy these underground passages that dated supposedly all the way back to the French-Indo China War.

Members of the new force were called Moles. An appropriate name because that's exactly what he felt like, lying on the cool dirt in total blackness. He could see nothing nor could he hear any sounds from within the tunnel itself. He lit a match to get his bearings. The entry chamber in which he found himself provided crawling room only. He noticed that it veered sharply to the right about ten feet in front of him. Watching a huge rat scuttle along the floor ahead of him, its hind claws scratching extra hard as it topped a slight swelling in the dirt, Spence smiled. Approaching the tiny rise in the ground, he expended another match. He recognized the object as an American-made claymore mine. Peering ahead, he stretched his legs till his feet touched the base of the cavern walls on both sides, and then he duck-walked over the explosive. After reaching the corner, he struck still another match. The jag in the tunnel proved to be short, leading to a larger room. Carefully picking his way along, Spence slid down an embankment into the next chamber. Another match revealed a small armory, lining the walls of the room.

He would have to get this information back to headquarters, and besides, he couldn't very well chase the soldier he had been following all the way to Hanoi, or wherever the tunnel ended. Being just as careful as he had been on his way in, he traced his way back to the entrance. He worried that he had stayed too long because he could not hear the whacking noise of the chopper blades above ground. The assault group must have moved out. He would have to hurry to catch up with them.

Stepping out of the tunnel into the open air, the bright sun played tricks with his eyes. He was temporarily blinded. His focus partly restored, he noticed blurred silhouettes surrounding him. Blinking and rubbing his eyes, he recognized them as Vietcong regulars, their guns trained at him.

For two days they kept him tied to a post in the center of their small village. Women and children spit on him and poked all over his body with sharp bamboo sticks. They fed him only a few mouthfuls of rice and gave him just a small cup of water. Passing soldiers jeered at him and encouraged the women and children to torment him further.

In the middle of the afternoon on the third day of his captivity, Spence welcomed a heavy rainstorm. It not only clenched his thirst, but it provided him with an opportunity to escape. After waiting for the rain to thoroughly drench the ground around him, Spence slowly wiggled the post to which he was tied. Little by little, he sensed it loosening in the mucky ground. Finally, he could raise it out of the mud entirely. Checking to see that no one was watching, he slid down the post till he sat on the ground, and finally slipped his hands off the end of it. Under the cover of the rain's blinding torrent, he had disappeared into the dense jungle, his hands still tied behind his back.

A familiar voice forced his mind back to the reality of his hopeless situation.

"Well, well, well, you're still hanging around," Jake laughed, patting Sandi under her chin. You mean to say your daddy didn't come in his private plane to bring you home? He should take better care of his pretty daughter, dont'cha think, Rafe?"

"Yeah, *I certainly would* if she was my daughter," Rafe agreed jokingly.

"I guess I'll just have to substitute for your daddy and give you what you need," Jake said.

"Wait a minute," Rafe grunted, walking over to Marna. "I don't want *my* girl thinking I've neglected her." He nudged her in the side with his foot. "I know we only went a third of the way around-the-world, but I need more time to get my juices flowing again. And besides, it's time for Jake to have a little fun. But don't you worry none 'cuz I'll be back soon enough."

Numbed with pain, Spence looked at Marna. She stared upward at the tree limbs above her, seemingly oblivious to what Rafe was saying to her. *If only now he were tied to a post instead of a tree, maybe he could free himself.*

"Okay, miss-rich-bitch, take one, scene two, or is it three? Oh, well, who cares, huh?" Jake stood in front of Sandi, holding a burning stick. "All my life, rich bitches like you snubbed me and wouldn't even give me the time of day, like I was so much dirt to be swept away. But *you* are different. You're gonna be nice to me and do exactly what I say. Right?"

Sandi had been hanging limp, her arms aching, her mind dazed. Eyes widening at the sight of the flaming stick before her, she balanced shakily on her toes, muffled screams coming through her gag.

"Like Rafe said to your friend, this is just to make sure I've got your full attention." Grabbing her by the hair, he jerked her head back and applied the torch to each of her breasts, sucking each one immediately after he singed them.

Even as he held her by the hair, she shook her head back and forth, her whole body convulsing.

"There, now, that wasn't so bad was it?" Jake said.

Rafe smiled as he sat on the ground watching excitedly, now and then swigging from his whiskey bottle.

"Now, you're one rich bitch who's gonna say ya love me for' we're through. See this switch," Jake said, brandishing a willowy branch before her fright-filled eyes. "My old man used to beat me with one like this. Only difference is he made me go into the woods and cut it for him. I've saved you that trouble. This is gonna sting like hell, but it'll teach you something, I hope. Bet your daddy never whipped that cute little ass of yours. Probably the only thing he ever put to it was baby powder. And that's mainly why you went astray and gave up your cherry to a guy you didn't even know. I'm gonna have to punish you for being so naughty."

He whipped her savagely on her back and buttocks, bloody welts appearing with each blow. He paused for a while, getting his breath. "Now tell me that you love me. Nod your head up and down, if you're ready to say that." Seeing no visible reaction, he continued to wallop her. Her head began to nod frantically.

Jake stepped around to face her. "I'm gonna remove your gag so you can tell me how much you love me." He pulled the gag away from her mouth without untying it in the back.

Tears flooding down her cheeks, she stammered, "I—I lo—ve yo—uu."

"Hear that, Rafe. This pretty rich bitch said she loves me." He put the gag back over her mouth, and stepping back he lashed her breasts twice. "Nod your head when you're ready to say *these* words: 'I want to suck your cock.'" He continued thrashing her, singing, *"A dog, a woman, and a walnut tree, the more you beat 'em, the better they be."*

Dizzy, the pain unbearable, her breasts laced with crimson stripes, Sandi consented and feebly nodded her head. His eyes gleaming, Jake lowered the rope till her knees rested on the ground. After anchoring the other end of the rope, he reached down and once more removed her gag.

*   *   *   *

Joe beached his canoe on the other side of Lake Alice. Disgruntled by the situation in which he found himself, he knew he would have to go along with it. It was not the first time he got into trouble with his older brother, but never anything as deep as murder. He had had brushes with the law, but nothing that would put him in prison for life. He considered running away. Maybe he could disappear for a while without finking on his brother, and yet keep himself from being an accomplice to murder. But all the good times he had with Rafe kept flashing through his mind, and he realized that as much as he hated to be a part of this crime, he would do what Rafe had told him to do. *In grade school, he had idolized his big brother, as he watched him score touchdown after touchdown as a fullback for Camdenton High School. He had proudly absorbed the comments from people around him in the stands. "That guy's a helluva fullback. He can name the college he wants to attend," one man said.*

"I heard he's even got pro scouts watching him already," another added.

"He's got a bright future. That's for sure, if he can avoid injuries," the other man continued.

His love for his brother had gone beyond football. Rafe had been his friend, confidant, and protector in those days. Anyone who messed with Joe would have Rafe to contend with. Consequently, no one ever had dared cause Joe any trouble.

Joe unloaded only part of the provisions from his canoe, setting out just what he would need for the night. He realized that he was taking a chance, by not tying all of the food packs in a tree, but thoughts of having to move out quickly prevailed. If bears or other animals rooted around the canoe, he would hear them and scare them away with a few shots from his revolver.

As he busied himself making camp, something moving out of the corner of his eye startled him. He turned his head quickly to see two men, paddling casually along the shoreline.

"Hello there," a stocky, full-bearded man yelled with a friendly wave of his hand. The man in the rear of the canoe, wearing a Cubs ball cap, smiled as he steered their canoe right along side of Joe's.

"Hi," Joe said, wondering what their conversation would bring.

They pulled into shore but didn't attempt to get out of their canoe.

"Looks like you're just setting up," the bearded man said. "Are you camping alone?"

Joe had the urge to get nasty, but he decided to play it safe, at least till he found out what they wanted. "No, I'm waiting for some friends of mine. Not sure exactly when they'll show up. Maybe later on tonight. You guys heading back to Ely?"

"Naw! We just got here two days ago. We'll probably stay about a week or so. A bunch of us come here fishing every few years. We're camped over two miles from here. Me and Bob have been checking out some fishing spots on the other side of this island. By the way, my name's Dan Gleason and this is Bob Adams. We're from Dubuque, Iowa. Ever heard of it?"

"Can't say that I have," Joe said, not volunteering his name.

"Have you been catching any fish?" Bob asked.

"Ah, no. We haven't done any fishing yet. Maybe when we get to our destination." He wished he hadn't said that. He was already uneasy with the conversation.

"Where are you headed?" Dan asked.

"Pretty far north from here."

"See you got a motor. Didn't know they were allowed in these waters," Dan said.

"Well, ah, you're right. They're not legal, but we got a special permit to use 'em because we work for the government. Our job is to check out these remote camps to see if they need any repairs and what not." Joe hoped he sounded convincing.

"Gees," Dan said, "I'd like a job like that. Sure beats working in a factory."

"Oh, it's got its ups and downs, like any other job," Joe responded, still being vague.

"Not to change the subject," Bob said, "but did you hear any strange noises over on this side of the island? We've been hearing off and on all day what sounds like girls' screams."

Joe tensed, beads of sweat forming on his forehead. What should he say? He'd have to be careful. "Oh, ah, yeah. I can explain that, I think. You see we've got some college girls working with us this summer. They're good workers, but sometimes they get a little crazy. If someone pours cold water down their back, they scream the same as if it was

boiling oil. Sometimes they get on my nerves with all their shrieking."
Joe hoped they would hear no cries at this time.

"Oh, that explains it then," Dan said, chuckling. "We actually thought someone might be in trouble of some sort. And we couldn't tell where the sounds were coming from. You know the way voices get distorted echoing across the water."

"We better be getting back to camp," Bob broke in. "The rest of the guys will think we drowned or something. We've been gone for about five hours."

"Yeah, you're right," Dan agreed. "Say, maybe we'll see you again tomorrow. There's a deep hole around the bend with a lot of hungry fish in it, if you're interested. I know some of our crew will probably want to test it out in the morning. We caught three big walleyes without even trying hard." He held up a stringer with the fish still flapping.

"So long," Joe said, relieved that they were finally moving out. "I doubt if we'll get much of a chance to fish in this area."

Watching them disappear around the bend in the island, Joe pondered over what he should do. His first impulse was to whip across the lake and tell those guys to hightail it before they were caught. But then he didn't want to witness the horrors he imagined were going on. And besides, they had insisted that he wait for them right where he was, and like it or not, that's what he would do. He'd give them till 4:30 in the morning. If they weren't there by then, he would fire three warning shots to hustle them up.

CHAPTER 12

▼

Spence watched helplessly as Jake mutilated Sandi's body, stabbing her again and again.

"Fuckin' whore bit me," Jake railed, looking down at the bloody corpse.

"And another one bites the dust," Rafe said, laughing at his own wit.

"C'mere, Rafe, and help me drag these two stiffs back into the woods. Fuckin' flies are driving me crazy. Besides, I gotta clear the stage for Blondie over there. I imagine she's getting anxious to do her part for our movie, 'specially since it'll be her final performance."

Spence knew it would be Marna's turn soon. Looking at her eyes staring blankly into the branches of the tree above her, he sensed that she had already resigned herself to death and simply was waiting for it to happen. Having watched the grim scenes acted out before him, he felt his own mind snapping. He expected his brain would explode before his body gave out. Never in all the torture that he had suffered in Vietnam had his mind become such a powder keg. He had watched as men were tortured before him, knowing it would be his turn next. He had felt close to death many times during the war. But he had vowed he would never "go gently into the good night." Death would not take him easily.

Watching the two men drag the bloody bodies of what were only yesterday young, vivacious girls, now infested with flies and ants, filled Spence with a rage of hatred and despair that he had never before experienced. War always gave rise to atrocities of all kinds. But this was not war. This was senseless slaughter of innocent lives. Brutal, sadistic mayhem. *And there was nothing he could do about it.*

After discarding the corpses in tall weeds about thirty feet from the tents, the two men returned.

"Jesus, I'm gonna take a swim to get rid of some of the stink," Jake said, wiping blood off his arms.

"Sounds like a good idea," Rafe said. "Then I'm gonna finish fucking around-the-world with Pussyhontas over there. I can tell she's getting excited again, and I'm horny as hell myself."

After swimming for ten minutes, Jake and Rafe traipsed up the path toward their captives.

"Help me string this blonde bitch up, 'for you get too weak from humping that other whore," Jake said.

"What are you gonna do to this one?"

"This is gonna be an exotic scene. I'll need her tied up *real good*. Saw it in a movie once. What the fuck was the name of it? Can't think of it now. Anyway this cowpoke tied up an Indian squaw and cut off one of her tits and made a tobacco pouch out of it. I've wanted a tit pouch ever since, and this bitch has got the nicest jugs I've ever seen." Jake enjoyed the look of horror in Julie's eyes, as he pressed his knife blade to one of her breasts.

*   *   *   *

By 9:45 p.m., a cool breeze wafted in from across the lake. Jake and Rafe sat at the table finishing off the last of their whiskey, their faces glimmering in the firelight. They had dumped Julie's body with the others.

"You're actually gonna make a pouch out of that thing," Rafe asked.

"Yep! Tomorrow I'll gut it out and tan it the same way you would an animal skin," Jake said, a smile on his lips. "If ya want, I'll make you one too."

"No, don't bother."

"Jesus, did ya see the way her body bucked when I started cutting? Didn't take long for the bitch to pass out. Lucky for her."

"Didn't take her long to bleed to death either," Rafe said, swigging from his bottle.

"Three down, two to go. Whatdya say we waste them and get the fuck out of here tonight. At least meet with your brother?"

"No! I want old soldier boy there to stew a little more. I want that tough fucker to taste fear 'for we're through with him."

"How you planning to snuff 'em?"

"I want him to watch her die first, then he gets it, slow and painful."

"That still doesn't tell me how the fuck you're gonna do it," Jake said exasperated.

"Well, fuck it! C'mere, I'll explain it to them too."

Walking over to Marna, Rafe kicked her in the side. "Wake up, slut. I gotta prepare you and your boyfriend for tomorrow's festivities. Jake, give him a boot to make sure he's listening."

"Happy to oblige," Jake said, viciously kicking Spence in the knee.

"Listen up, you two," Rafe said. "Tomorrow you're gonna die, bright and early. And this is the way it's goin' down. First, I'm gonna roast this fuckin' whore of yours, soldier. But only for a while till the wood burns down, then she'll hang, and you get to watch her dance on the end of a rope just to make sure we do it proper. Then, of course, you get the same kind of treatment. Are there any objections? No— then I guess that's it till dawn. Sleep well!"

"Let me check their ropes, Rafe. I want to make sure they stick around till morning. I'd hate to have them miss this action, the final scene in our movie. Haw! Haw!"

*   *   *   *

When dawn broke, Spence witnessed the first signs of activity in the camp. Rafe ambled out of a tent and started a fire. He put on a pot of coffee, and when it was ready, he roused Jake. Spence had suffered through the night, waiting for some kind of miracle that he knew wouldn't happen. He had wished that he could at least talk to Marna. Somehow soften the impending torture. He had desperately tried all night to loosen his ropes; they were not quite as tight as before, but he had a long way to go before he could free himself.

Seeing the darkness spill over into the morning light and hearing the first bird chirp, Spence knew that death was imminent. He could smell it. His own death he could face, but to watch Marna suffer unspeakable pain, he couldn't bear. *Yet he knew he must.* He had watched her writhe on the ground all night long, her naked body chilled by the cool night air. He wondered what her thoughts might be. Was she still coherent after what they had already done to her? Or had her mind snapped? Was she already in that twilight world between life and death, not conscious of reality?

Spence eyed the two killers as they gathered firewood. They built two piles directly in front of him. After they had stacked the wood to about three feet high, they threw a rope around an overhanging limb and fashioned a hangman's noose on the dangling end.

"Well, well, well, my little Pussyhontas, you were a good fuck while you lasted, but your days of fuckin' have come to an end," Rafe said, staring down at Marna. "To the end of a rope, that is, 'less the fire gets you first. I'm not exactly sure how this will work, not having done it before. Hey, soldier, watch carefully 'cuz you get to try it next." He bent over to cut Marna's bonds. Jake approached with the can of gasoline.

"Should I douse her too, Rafe?"

"No! Just sprinkle a little around the wood at the bottom. We want it to go nice and slow. Right?"

"Sure thing," Jake said, unscrewing the lid.

Before Rafe cut even one rope, anchoring Marna to the ground, three shots echoed across the lake.

"What the fuck was that?" Jake shouted.

"How the fuck do I know?" Rafe yelled back at him. "It must be Joe warning us. What else could it be?"

"Let's waste 'em and get the fuck outta here," Jake snapped. I'll just plug 'em both between the eyes. *Better yet*, these two belong to you. So far *I've* done all the killing." Holding the gun by the barrel, he passed it over to Rafe who nervously took it in his hands.

Pointing the gun shakily at Spence whose eyes were nearly closed, Rafe snarled, "If you make it to Hell, fucker, tell 'em Rafe sent ya." He hoped his words concealed his obvious tension as he jerkily fired two quick shots. He turned away as one hit Spence's skull, knocking his head against the tree, blood pouring from the wound. The other bullet penetrated his chest.

His hands still quivering, Rafe aimed at Marna and fired. The hammer clicked. He desperately pulled the trigger two more times. Two more clicks. "Out of fucking bullets," he growled, looking toward Jake.

"It don't matter. She's already dead. Look at her fucking eyes."

"Okay." A look of relief passed over Rafe's face. "Let's cut their ropes and drag them back with the rest. And, if we hide the tents too, maybe no one will find 'em for a few days."

After covering Marna's body with weeds, they disposed of Spence in the same manner. Then they hurriedly flung the tents behind tall bushes. Within twenty minutes, they were hightailing it across Lake Alice, their engine wide open.

CHAPTER 13

▼

The early morning sun shimmering off their giant black wings, vultures circled lazily in the azure sky. Slowly they tightened their flying pattern and lowered it closer to the earth. One by one they glided in for a landing, and after touching down with a flapping of their huge wings, they paraded toward a clump of thick bushes. Their bald heads bobbed from side to side, as they cautiously checked for any imminent dangers. The lead bird warily approached the first body, pausing long enough to carefully scrutinize the surrounding terrain, then pecked several times at the fly-infested bloody flesh. The red morsels, dangling from his beak, seemed to be the signal for the others to join him in the feast.

Twenty buzzards in all congregated at the scene. Some perched on low branches of nearby pine trees, seemingly content to serve as sentinels for their ravenous brethren. The rest gorged themselves on morsels of plentiful flesh. They hopped and fluttered from one corpse to another, sometimes fighting over the same stringy bit of meat, strange shrill noises emitting from their elongated throats.

Spence awakened to a vulture pecking methodically at the open wound in his chest. *In his unconscious state, he had found himself walking down a long, narrow, and highly illuminated corridor. Misty vapors obscured the end of the tunnel. Familiar faces appearing in the haze, beck-*

oned for him to cross the murky chasm that separated them. No words had been spoken, but he knew they were calling him to join them on the other side. He felt so peaceful and happy, but as he walked slowly, narrowing the gap between them, other visages more dominating than the rest, motioned him to stay back.

Opening his eyes and seeing the wretched carnivorous bird feeding on his flesh made him realize that he was still alive. Excruciating pain, pounding in his head, stabbing at his chest, and coursing throughout his whole body confirmed that sensation. *He was alive.*

Mustering what little strength remained in his body, Spence slowly raised his hands, fragments of rope hanging from his wrists, and clutched the buzzard by its neck. Flapping its wings, it tried desperately to fly away while at the same time its talons raked viciously into Spence's chest, making deep gashes. Screeching as it lapsed into its death throes, red eyes bulging from their sockets, one of its legs lashed out, the claws slicing crimson furrows across Spence's cheek. Squeezing the limp neck firmly till he was sure that the vulture was dead, Spence gradually released the pressure, finally allowing the ugly, lifeless creature to topple on to the ground.

Spence lay still, breathing as deeply as the pain in his chest would allow. He sensed that the rest of the buzzards were becoming wary as a result of the death struggle. In a flurry of flapping wings, several flew to the trees for safety. The others dined more nervously, hopping to a safer distance to consume the bloody scraps protruding from their mouths.

Painstakingly, Spence assessed the damage to his body. The claw marks he ignored. How many times had he been shot? And would any of his wounds be fatal? Putting his hands to his head, he traced his fingers through his blood-soaked hair to where one bullet had penetrated the left side of his skull and to the spot where it had exited. Either it had ricocheted off bone or the guy was a poor marksman. But for whatever reason, it had not entered his brain. The bastards must have gone or the buzzards would never have landed. Moving his hands down to his chest, he fingered the bullet hole, surmising that the bullet had lodged inside him. Painful though the wound was and still seeping blood, he sensed that no vital organs had been damaged.

But what about Marna? Where was she? What had they done to her? He let his head sag to the side where the vultures continued to feast. He saw her body five feet away. Two of those hideous creatures plucked at her flesh.

"Get away from her," he cried, pain shooting through his head, tears filling his eyes. Too weak to stand, he slowly forced his body to a sitting position, his back resting against a birch tree. Spotting a dead branch between him and Marna, he crawled toward it. Falling on his side, he rolled over to the club. He gripped it in both hands, and, using it as a support, he struggled on his knees toward Marna. The two buzzards changed their positions as Spence awkwardly approached, but they didn't fly away. When he got within range, he jabbed the stick at one of the birds' head, poking out an eye. Blood oozing from the socket, the vulture spread its huge wings and flew to a tree, screeching in pain. The other backed off, but not far enough. Spence smashed the bird's head, killing it instantly. Shaking wings wildly and shrieking in fright, the entire flock flew skyward, deprived of their banquet.

Fatigued from the battle, Spence collapsed next to Marna. *At least he had saved her body for a decent funeral,* he thought, tears streaming down his cheeks. He lay there for a long time, trying to regain his strength. The murdering bastards had made a costly mistake. They had left him for dead in their rush to escape. They would pay the price for their carelessness as soon as he was able to track them down. He would have to bandage his wounds before losing too much blood. *Survival before vengeance.* Because of his weakened condition, he could not make it back to his canoe and certainly not back to his campsite across Lake Alice. He would have to scrounge around the camp and see what provisions might have been left.

Convincing himself that he was ready to drag his body to the tents, he rose to a sitting position, and for the first time, observed the carnage before him. The bloody, partly eaten remains of what were four beautiful women made his guts heave. He retched again and again, bile burning his throat and chest. As he leaned on one elbow off to the side to make vomiting easier, he heard sounds which at first he mistakenly thought had come from his own body, but then he realized the groans had come from Marna.

Bending over her, he pulled down her gag. She murmured. How could it be that she was alive too? "Marna! Marna!" He cried. "Can you hear me?" When she did not respond immediately, he checked her for vital signs. Her pulse beat fairly steady, her breathing becoming easier by the second. He examined her naked body from her head to her feet. No deep wounds of any kind that he could notice. What made them think she was dead? But then he realized that he had believed her to be dead too. She must have become comatose from fear or shock. He had witnessed similar situations in Vietnam. Just when they were about to slip what all thought to be a dead soldier into a body bag, he would recover from a coma and start mumbling and wonder what was happening to him.

Spence called Marna's name again, this time shaking her gently. Her eyes that had been staring fixedly blinked several times. "S-S-ppp-ee-nnce," she murmured.

"Thank, God!" He kissed her softly on her forehead, her cheek, and finally on the lips. "I'll get you some water. It'll take me a while since I can't move very fast. But don't worry. I'll be back."

His energy renewed, Spence hobbled to the hidden tents, using the branch as a crutch. Finding several towels and torn sweatshirts, he fashioned bandages for his wounds, tying them tight enough to curtail the bleeding. Taking a plastic glass and another towel from one of the overnight bags, he painstakingly made his way to the lake. After clenching his own thirst, he stumbled up the path toward Marna.

As he dabbed at her face with the wet towel, she smiled feebly. He lifted her head to give her a drink, happy to see that she was coming out of her stupor. Noticing a worried look in her eyes, he comforted her by assuring her that the men were gone for good.

"Julie? Sue? Sandi? What about them?"

"Dead."

On his trek for water, Spence had found the can of gasoline that the butchers had left behind. The wood, intended for use in their cruel, inhuman form of torture would be the right amount for the fire he was going to light. After assisting Marna to the shade of a large tree, he joined the two piles of wood in an opening among the trees and soaked the pyre with gasoline. He threw a hot coal from the breakfast fire on to the brush and watched it ignite into a ball of fire. Despite his pain, he was able to drag a sleeping bag down to the lake for a good dousing. He dropped it onto the fire, smothering the flames. Peeling it back quickly, he allowed a puff of smoke to escape and billow skyward. He repeated this operation several times, hoping the rangers close to the town of Ely would see his signal.

An hour later, huddling with Marna in the shade, Spence heard the sounds of a pontoon plane as it banked before coming in for a landing on Lake Alice.

"We're gonna make it!" he said, stroking Marna's hair.

CHAPTER 14

▼

Spence struggled frantically, trying to loosen the ropes that bound him to a tree. His naked body soaked, sweat mingling with blood seeping from his open wounds, he cursed himself for his carelessness. Getting caught was his only sin, but he knew he would suffer for his mistake and so would the others.

Several fires in the camp illuminated patches of darkness and burned away the mist from the steamy nighttime jungle. Men and women penned up in tiger cages, horror-stricken, screamed as guards prodded them with sharp bamboo sticks.

Ominous shadows passed in and out of the firelight, as giant birds looking like pterodactyls swooped out of the jungles screeching, "Awk! Awk! Awk!" Their eyes, burning hot coals that served as headlights penetrating the darkness.

Agonizing screams pierced the night, as the Vietcong dragged their prisoners out of their cages to be tortured. Spence strained against his ropes over and over. He had to get loose to save the others from merciless slaughter. But the ropes would not slacken. He was bound too tightly. The more that he struggled, the deeper the ropes cut into his bleeding flesh. Nausea overwhelmed him. Helpless and ashamed, he could only watch the grisly scene unfold before him.

The Vietcong hung their first victim by his wrists over a fire. The flames licked and lapped at his naked body, his legs kicking wildly. Animalistic howls of pain emitted from his blackened throat terrifying all the prisoners. The stench of charred flesh filled the air, gagging Spence. They tied another soldier to a post and broke his bones by smashing him with the butt of a rifle. Spence winced at each cracking sound. The man's screams turned to shrieks till he passed out from the agony. Then they continued to pound his limp body, squashing the life out of him.

Spence stared in horror as the ruthless soldiers dragged one of the women from her cage. She fought them with all her strength—but in vein. They ripped her clothes from her body as they forced her toward the center of the camp, pulling her hair and shoving her brutally till she stumbled and fell to the ground. Crawling on hands and knees, she painfully made her way to her place of torture.

"My God," Spence screamed. "It's Marna." Don't you hurt her anymore, you fuckin' butchers." A guard slammed him in the side of the head with his rifle, stunning him. Slowly opening his eyes, Spence saw soldiers milling around their victim. His stomach churned at the sight of Marna, spread-eagled on the ground, her hands and feet tied to stakes—her face battered and bloody. A tall redheaded man stood naked over her, fondling his huge penis that protruded from his body—a weapon, poised to tear her insides apart.

"Okay, bitch! You're mine!" His sweaty, naked body shimmering in the firelight, he pounced on top of her.

"No! No!" Spence screamed as the soldier rammed his manhood into Marna's twisting, turning body. Spence exerted every ounce of strength in his already weakened muscles, desperately trying to break loose and go to Marna's aid. She pleaded for him to help her.

"Spence! Spence!" she cried.

Spence wept at the sight of that brute pumping up and down on her body.

When the man with the flaming red hair had finished taking her, he turned her over to the other soldiers who, with sickening smirks on their faces, took turns with her. One bit into her right breast and spit blood and flesh into her face. Another beat her face savagely with his fists. Each one sadistically tortured her in his own way. When they had all been satisfied, her body lay in a lifeless heap upon the ground. Tears streamed down Spence's face as he watched—totally helpless. Spence's eyes widened, horror filled as he recognized their next victim. Julie's long, blond hair glistened in the light of the fire. Her blood curdling screams drowned out her assailants' jeering laughter as they repeatedly raped her. Then one of the soldiers hacked her to death with a machete, his final swing lopping off her head which rolled over to Spence's feet, gore dripping from the severed arteries, the eyes staring balefully at Spence. A huge bird, its eyes fiery red, swooped in low and clutched the bloody head in its talons and then flapped into the night, screeching triumphantly.

Grotesque faces surrounded Spence, jeering and cursing him as they closed in to torture him. Through an open space in the crowd, he noticed Marna feebly struggling to free herself. "Marnaaaa-aaa!" he cried, as he slipped into a dark void, straining against his bonds, his body aching. The evil faces of his tormentors gradually faded away; only pain and darkness remained. He tossed and turned in misery for what seemed like hours till a dim light burned through the shadows. At first it was very faint, but eventually it beamed brighter.

A distorted face appeared in the glow. Fearing that his captors had returned, he cringed momentarily. A blurred vision of Marna's bloody face hovered over him. He squinted, trying desperately to bring her features into focus.

"Marna," he whispered, attempting to lift his body toward her.

A gentle but firm hand pressed on his chest forcing him down. "There now! It's okay. You're safe. You've just had surgery and you're going to be all right." Marna's tortured face slowly disappeared, as Spence looked into the eyes of the sweet young nurse whose voice was kind and reassuring.

Blinking his eyes, he glanced about the room. "Where am I? And where is Marna? Is she okay?" His throat felt dry and his voice sounded raspy.

"You're in Minneapolis General Hospital—and don't worry, Marna's going to be all right too. She's almost right above you on the next floor," the nurse said, putting the straw from the water glass to his lips.

"I want to see her," Spence commanded, after taking a sip of water to soothe his parched throat.

"Well, now, recovering enough to give orders, are you? That's a good sign, but I'm afraid it'll be a couple of days before you're strong enough to move about. You lost a lot of blood. And besides, Marna needs her rest too."

"How long have we been here?"

"Four days," the nurse replied.

Spence only remembered bits and pieces of those days. After boarding the National Guard copter at Ely, he had passed out. He came to in the emergency room just before his operation.

"Do you mean I've been out since the operation?"

"You've had *several* operations. The last one was to set your multiple-fractured ribs."

Spence could feel the tape job. His body ached with the slightest movement. He remembered vividly parts of his nightmare, and he tried to sort out what had been a dream and what had actually happened to him and the girls in the Boundary Waters. Those murdering bastards. They would not get away with it. They had butchered three beautiful women and had left Marna and him for dead. *That was a very bad mistake on their part.* There was no place in the world that they could hide from him. Killing them would be easy—too easy maybe. But then Spence knew of ways to prolong dying. He had seen men beg to be killed in Nam. He himself had come close to that cowardly indignity. Afterall, he had been tortured by experts—and he could never forget their methods. They seemed to know just how much a human body could stand before it expired. The mind always went first, but the body suffered pain all the way to the end. The body writhed in agony long after signs of anything human in spirit had left it.

He would skin that red headed bastard alive for what he had done. Maybe that would satisfy for the others too. He had observed soldiers being skinned. The carving away of layers of skin proved painful beyond belief. But it was the exposed flesh and nerve fibers that were so sensitive to even the slightest touch. A heated blade applied with the precision of a master torturer guaranteed agony that reached to the very depths of Hell and back.

There were so *many* ways to torment those butchers to death. They would beg to be killed all right, before he would send them on their way—*not so* "gently into that good night."

*   *   *   *

The three men trudged along the lane that supposedly led to a cabin. Joe Johnson walked beside his brother Rafe. Jake Green trailed them by a few feet. They were relieved to be in the shade of the dense forest out of the hot afternoon sun. The old whiskered man at the station in town had given them specific directions.

"Follow the main road till ya come to two big rocks on the right side. Between them's a wide path that'll take ya to your uncle's place." He had chatted excitedly, giving them more information than they cared to hear.

"What are we gonna tell Uncle Louie?" Joe asked, rubbing his thumbs under the pack straps that dug into his shoulders.

"As little as possible," Rafe answered quickly. "No sense in getting him all riled up. Besides, he might turn us in if he thought there was any reward money to be had. He's a cagey bastard, if I remember him right."

"Ya think he'll grubstake us till things cool down some?" Jake asked.

"Hope so," Rafe said. "Our cash is running out."

The grassy makeshift road winding through the forest stretched to over two miles like the old guy had said it would. As they rounded a bend, the cabin came into view. A small lake surrounded by pine trees extended almost to the front porch. A little girl with long black hair swung back and forth in a tree swing. Seeing the strangers approach her, she dragged her feet till the swing slowed down enough for her to jump off. She ran toward the cabin, a startled look on her face. Shortly after she disappeared into the cabin, an Indian woman, cradling a shotgun in her arms, stepped onto the porch.

"Is that your Uncle Louie's squaw?" Jake whispered, a smile spreading over his face.

"Be dammed if I know," Rafe said. "We'll find out soon enough, *if she doesn't blow us away.*"

"Afternoon, Ma'am," Joe said cheerfully, as the three men paused a short distance from the cabin. "We're looking for Louie Broussard. I'm his nephew, Joe, and this is my brother Rafe, and our friend Jake."

The woman said nothing as she studied the three men. The little girl peeked through the screen door, a worried look on her face.

"My husband is not home," the woman said sternly.

"Well, ah, do you know when he'll be back?" Rafe asked.

"Soon," she said.

"Can we set our packs down and get a drink—and, ah, wait outside here for him?" Rafe asked.

"That'll be okay I guess. There's a pump out on this side of the cabin," she said, pointing to her left with the gun barrel.

The men slowly eased their packs to the ground beneath a blue spruce. They nodded at the woman as they passed her. By the time they had gotten a drink and cooled off by pouring water over their heads, she had gotten rid of her gun and had busied herself cleaning fish on a table in the shade of a pine tree. Her daughter had returned to her swing.

The men watched in silence as the woman skillfully cleaned and gutted the mess of walleyes. Occasionally, she waved her butcher knife menacingly at the horde of flies that had invaded the bloody guts. After filleting the fish, she carried most of them to a small log building that served as a smokehouse. The rest of the fish she dumped into a metal dishpan and carted them into the cabin. The sound of a truck grinding its gears alerted the three men. They watched as a blue Ford pick-up stopped in front of the cabin.

A heavily bearded man stepped out of the truck. "What kin I do for you guys?" he asked, his voice friendly with a French accent.

"Uncle Louie," Rafe said, offering his hand. "You don't remember me, do you?"

"Well, by god! You must be Rafe. I haven't seen you in ten years or more," Louie said, shaking Rafe's hand firmly. "What brings you up this way?"

"We need a vacation—sort of," Rafe said, hesitating. The look in his uncle's eyes told him that Louie knew it was a *forced vacation*.

"Could ya use any extra hands on your loggin' crew? We're a little short of money."

"Ah, not really. Just hired two new guys last week. Good workers. But I'll tell you what I'll do. I'll pay the going rate for one man, and you can split it three ways, or the other two can try their luck somewhere else."

"Sounds okay to me," Rafe said. "What about you guys?"

Jake and Joe nodded, but their eyes showed they were unconvinced that it was such a good deal.

"I'll throw in a cabin free. You can stay there as long as you want. It's down the main road about three miles—almost on the other side of the lake. Ain't much, but it'll keep you warm and dry. This must be little Joe—all growed up," Louie said, extending his hand.

"That's right, and this is Jake Green," Joe said.

"Met my wife and daughter, I 'spose," Louie said, looking toward the cabin.

"Sorta," Rafe said. "I think they were a little afraid of us at first. But then I don't much blame 'em. We've been camping out for some time, and we look pretty grubby."

"Well," Louie said, "let's have a few beers then you kin clean up 'fore supper." The three of them followed Louie into the cabin.

*   *   *   *

Spence stared out the window of his hospital room. Three days had passed, and he still had not been allowed to see Marna. Whenever he would ask about her, he was told that she was doing fine, and he could see her when he was well enough. Waiting another full two days, he got the same run-a-round. But that nonsense was about to end. He would go that night to see Marna after the next shift of nurses made their routine check of patients. He had noticed the closet where the orderlies picked up their clean uniforms. He knew that he could get there easily without being seen. Dressed in green, he would simply take the stairs to the next floor. He had remembered the nurse who had unwittingly revealed that Marna rested in a room almost directly above him. That narrowed things down somewhat. He had a general destination anyway. If he didn't locate her room within a reasonable time through trial and error, he would simply go to the desk on the next floor and try to spot the room listings without any hassle. He would have to think of a plan if it got down to that. Maybe the nurse at the desk would leave her post for a minute to get coffee or something. *Just maybe he would get that lucky.*

They had fooled him temporarily by not listing her name and room at the main desk. He had called on his room phone thinking it would be so easy. But they were on to him. Why would they care so much whether or not he saw her? After all they had suffered together, they had a right to see one another. He didn't want to upset her or anything. Just talk to her and hold her. Hell, it would be good therapy for both of them. She must be feeling better with all of the care and rest.

Hadn't he been in worse shape? And he felt stronger by the day. He wondered if Marna was trying to reach him too—and getting the same red-tape treatment.

After the evening meal, Spence entered the closet where the uniforms were stored. He dressed as quickly as his sore ribs would allow and then listened intently for sounds outside the door. Hearing nothing out of the ordinary, he swung the door open and walked down the dimly lit, gray tiled hallway. He strolled casually as if he were in no particular hurry. Upon reaching the door to the staircase, he exited without even turning his head to avoid suspicion. His heart beat a little faster till he stood outside the door checking through the glass window to see if he had been followed. Confident that he was safe so far, he hurried up the stairs to the next floor. Pausing at the door, he jerked it open and strode to his right down the hallway. He had mentally figured out where Marna's room would be in relation to his on the floor below. Farther down the corridor he observed a nurse entering a room with a pitcher of ice water. He knew she would not be long, so he slowed his pace checking several rooms as he walked. A quick glance into each one told him what he wanted to know. All the rooms so far had contained two patients. He assumed Marna would be in a private room as he had been, due to the nature of her injuries.

Passing the nurse who had been making her rounds, he smiled slightly and tried to hide his fear. She barely responded as she disappeared into another room.

After frantically checking several more rooms on either side of the hallway, beads of sweat popped out of Spence's brow. Someone was bound to ask him what he was searching for. That would give him away for certain. He sensed that the staff had been warned about his desperate attempts at visiting Marna during regular hours. For some reason they remained steadfast in keeping him and Marna apart.

He had to think of something fast. Rounding a bend in the corridor, he was startled to see a nurse sitting at a desk flipping through several papers. She glanced up and smiled. Spence continued toward her in what he hoped was a purposeful gait, his mind reeling. He would have to play his cards sooner than he had wanted to. "Hi," he blurted with a quick wave of his hand. "Maybe I can get some help at last. I was called to prep a patient by the name of Greg Winters for early surgery tomorrow. I was told he was in Room 307, but he isn't. Could you check his number for me? I'd hate to shave the wrong guy."

"Sure, just a sec," she said, running her finger down the list of names on a pad before her. Spence checked each name as she perused the list. "No one by that name on this floor. Are you sure they said third floor?"

"Yep," Spence answered, smug in knowing that Marna was listed in 324.

"I'll call the main desk and see what's going on," the nurse offered, as she tapped out numbers with a pen.

Spence waited patiently, knowing what she'd find out.

"Hello, this is Janet calling from third. Do you have a Greg Winters listed as a patient?" She smiled warmly at Spence, and shrugged, all the while drumming her fingers on her desktop.

"Are you sure?" She finally asked, a puzzled expression on her face. "Okay, thanks." Looking apologetically at Spence, she said, "No Greg Winters listed in the entire hospital. Must be some mistake."

"I think I've been had," Spence said. "One of the other orderlies has played a dirty trick on me, and I swallowed it all. Sorry to have bothered you. I feel so embarrassed. You won't tell anyone, will you?" he asked with a grin on his face.

"My lips are sealed," she said laughing.

Spence smiled and gave her a mock blessing. After rounding the bend in the corridor, he quickened his pace. Somehow he had gone the wrong way when he had entered the third floor via the stairs. He had just missed Marna's room off to the left. His pulse quickened as he almost bumped into a nurse hurrying from a room. She was the same one he had passed in the hallway before. She merely blinked recognition and continued speedily on her way—seemingly caught up in her duties.

The door to Room 324 was closed—unlike the other rooms. Spence wasted no time opening it and creeping toward Marna's bed. He stood above her, puzzled at the tangle of tubes and wires attached to her body. The faint glow from the monitor gave her face an eerie look, her eyes wide-open staring toward the ceiling.

"Marna?" he whispered softly, sweat beading on his brow. "Can you hear me? It's me, Spence. Remember me?"

No response. Her eyes stared fixedly. Spence touched her hair and bent down and kissed her gingerly on the cheek. Her body felt cold to his touch. He recognized one of the tubes connected to her wrist. She was being fed intravenously. But why? She must be strong enough to eat by herself. And why was she wired to that machine? The monotonous blipping seemed to be getting fainter as he looked at the screen. He glanced back at Marna. No visible change. The blips became more infrequent and of less magnitude. Spence couldn't believe what was happening. It couldn't be. He reached down and felt her pulse. Nothing registered. The faint blips stopped—swallowed by a straight buzzing line across the screen. An alarm sounded.

"Code Blue in Room 324," a voice echoed in the corridor.

Spence, terrified, pressed his lips to Marna's, and pinching her nostrils he gave her mouth-to-mouth resuscitation, oblivious to the crew of nurses and doctors who rushed into the room. Firm hands pulled him away from Marna and steered him across the room. He watched, dazed, as a nurse clamped electrical shock pads to Marna's chest. The resulting thumps caused Marna's body to jerk spasmodically. Spence winced at each jolt. Tears streaming down his cheeks, he stood there like a zombie. She would make it, he tried to convince himself. She had to make it—*for his sake.* She had survived her ordeal on the island. He had talked to her. She was in control of herself. A little care and rest was all she needed. What happened to her? If only he had found her room sooner, maybe he could have saved her. Maybe if she had seen him, she would have pulled through. What was he thinking? She was going to be all right. She had to be. She was the only one in the last ten years who made him want to live again—to look forward to tomorrow.

The emergency team kept their eyes glued to the monitor. The straight line on the scope never quivered. The doctor in charge shook his head back and forth. The nurse, about to apply the shock pads one more time, stopped and put them back on the emergency cart.

The three nurses and the two doctors looked toward Spence whom they had recognized, sadness in their eyes. "I'm sorry," one doctor said.

"No!" Spence cried, a low moaning at first. "No-o-o-o." His voice pierced the quiet of the room. It rose to shrieking sobs—more animal than human, as they resounded out of the room and down the corridors, terrifying nurses and patients alike. "She-e-e-'s no-o-o-t d-e-e-a-a-d! How can she be *dead*? She was alive! I talked to her! How could she die?"

One of the doctors approached him to offer a comforting hand to his shoulder. Spence slapped his hand away and rushed past the nurses to Marna. He ripped off all of the tubes and wires connected to her. Bending down, he picked up Marna's lifeless body, her eyes still wide-open and glassy. He hugged her tightly, sobbing, and murmuring incoherent sounds.

CHAPTER 15

▼

The afternoon sun felt good on Spence's back, as he walked slowly toward the door of the rustic cabin. His friend Ducky had said he could use the place as long as he wanted. It served as a hunting lodge for Ducky and his cronies during the winter months, and only rarely did they use it during the summer. Tucked away deep in the forest, nestling in between two densely wooded hills, the hide-a-way provided the kind of solitude Spence needed. Ducky had even thrown in his Ford pick-up so he could get to town whenever he wanted, but Spence was not in any hurry for company. He had lots to sort out in his mind, while he recuperated. He was relieved to be out of that hospital. He had gotten his emotions under control after the night Marna had died, and he had become hysterical. Both doctors and nurses had treated him kind of funny for a while. He had noticed how often they peered into his room at odd hours of the day and night without actually talking to him. They had been checking up on him. When they did talk to him, their words were guarded. None of the flippant remarks that the nurses had shot at him earlier in the week. They didn't want to upset him—touch him off—send him into that rage again.

Realizing that they would keep him in the hospital longer—maybe even attempt to have him confined in a mental ward—Spence played their game. Gradually, he convinced them by his behavior and conversation that he was stable; his mind had not snapped completely—only temporarily. He had behaved normally under the cruel circumstances. *At least that is what he wanted them to believe, so that he would be released without delay.* His ploy had worked. One week later, the doctor had said he could leave the hospital, provided he didn't do anything foolish to aggravate his wounds or overtax his body. If that doctor had only known his vengeful intentions, he never would have consented to his release.

The police had visited him several times during the week before his departure, asking him the same questions over and over again, as if they expected him to change his story. They almost seemed disappointed when he continued to tell them the same gory facts. It hadn't surprised him when they said they had no leads as to the whereabouts of the murderers. Spence had been careful not to give them accurate descriptions of the killers, pretending that he had been blindfolded most of the time or unconscious. They had somehow escaped a dragnet on both sides of the border. The Boundary Waters offered easy refuge for people to lose themselves, Spence reasoned. Very simple. Hole up on a secluded island by day and travel by night. He was glad those butchers had escaped. No prison for them with three squares a day and a place to roost. They were going to pay for their atrocities all right— more than they would ever think humanly possible. He would find them, if it took him the rest of his life. They would not be safe anywhere on this planet. Marna and the others would be avenged. *And so would he.*

It was still difficult for him to accept Marna's death. Dwelling on his hatred for her murderers helped him to push the sadness he felt out of his heart and mind. There had been nights in the hospital that he had allowed himself to wallow in self-pity. It was getting to the point where he enjoyed the feeling and the tears that accompanied it. He hadn't experienced emotions like that since he was a kid. Not even in Vietnam, where he had suffered so many torments, where his mind reeled daily, confronting a myriad of emotions new to him, did he feel sorry for himself. And it certainly was *himself* that he dwelled on. Marna was dead. She suffered no more pain, so it was not for her that he found himself in crying jags.

What kind of a hold did she have on him anyway. He had barely known her a week. The deaths of the other women didn't affect him the same. Was it love? He had not known her long enough to call it *love*. Could it have become love? Somehow Marna had given him a reason to go on living, a purpose in seeing a new day through. For the past several years he had been just going through the motions of living, plodding through one day at a time without many real highs or lows. Knowing her made him think that his life could have taken on new meaning. But she was gone forever. And now he better understood the grief of the narrator in Poe's "The Raven" who kept asking the raven if he would ever see his beloved Lenore again, and the mysterious bird croaked only one word for an answer: "Nevermore."

Spence still had to come to grips with that horrible thought. Marna was gone from his life as quickly as she had entered it, and she was never coming back. That kind of reasoning made him consider suicide. One bullet to his brain would bridge the gap real easy between him and Marna. The cold reality of that fact had haunted him during his stay in the hospital. *It would be so damn easy.* What did he have to live for now? And maybe that's the same realization he would have arrived at on his solitary trek into the Boundary Waters, even if he had not met Marna. One flick of a trigger and it would be all over. *Maybe that was the answer.* The ultimate in living life was death, wasn't it? Maybe his friends who had committed suicide had the inside track. At least they found out sooner what went on beyond the grave.

There had been times in Vietnam when he had considered taking his own life, especially when the enemy had tortured him. He had watched several of his buddies kill themselves when the going got tough and they were about to be captured. And in some ways he had envied them. They couldn't suffer anymore. They were beyond pain. But then something would well up inside him. Fear of the unknown.

Hate for the enemy. *Whatever it was* made him want to live, to stick
around for the whole ride no matter what the consequences.

And that certain gut feeling overwhelmed him again. He was not
ready to check out of this life—not yet. He had some killing to do first,
and then maybe he would consider death as the only solution to his
misery. And that was the way he would leave it. No room for tears or
self pity—just hate for those bastards who had done him wrong. Hate
would be the driving force that would enable him to find them and
make them suffer for the evil they had wrought.

Turning the key in the lock, Spence stepped inside the cabin to a
spacious and comfortable looking haven. A large brick fireplace loomed
on the wall opposite the doorway, the head of a moose serving as sentinel above it. A bear rug stretched on the floor, its glassy eyes staring
fiercely. The place was better than he had expected. He sauntered to
the kitchen area and opened the refrigerator door. Ducky had stocked
it with enough food and beer to last a couple of weeks. That guy
thought of everything. He would have to repay him somehow, even
though Ducky didn't expect payment. The place would do just fine till
he recovered enough to embark on his seek-and-destroy mission.

The next morning the ax blade glistened in the sun as it reached the
apex of its arc above Spence's head. *Thunk* sounds echoed through the
hills as he split the log which stood upright on a flat, ground-level
stump. Spence wiped sweat from his forehead with the back of his
hand, before positioning the two halves for quartering. He was pleased
that he found a way to repay Ducky without insulting him. He would
get downright mad if Spence offered him money, even if he paid only
half of what it cost to put him up for a few weeks in the cabin.

He would chop enough wood to last Ducky and his pals the entire
winter. He could claim it was part of his training program—and in a
way it was. Each time the sharp ax sliced through a log, Spence envisioned the head of one of the murderers. It would be like chopping
meat in a butcher shop. No compassion. No mercy. They were dead
men. He had learned from his ordeal. How soft he had become since

he had landed Stateside after Nam. Being soft in Nam could cost you your life, and being soft in the Boundary Waters had cost *four lives* and nearly did him in too. How many times had he rerun that rescue mission through his brain. There were so many things he should have done differently. If only he had another chance, those girls might be alive, and Marna and he.... He had to forget it. Marna was dead. And her murderers were as good as dead too.

Spence sometimes wondered what the three of them were doing. He could see them chugging down beer in a bar some place in Canada, having good times like nothing had happened to them. And really nothing had happened to them *yet*. They would stay in Canada hiding out for as long as they thought necessary. And that was okay. He was in no rush. They would keep for the time being. He needed a few weeks to strengthen his body—to get himself as close to the shape he had been in as a member of the Special Forces in Nam. It would take some doing because of his age, his injuries, and the easy life he had been living. *But now he was at war again.* And he would prepare himself for battle. No slip-ups this time around. Those suckers were as good as dead. But they were going to know *how* they died. They would experience every second of their death. They would beg to die. And he would savor every moment of their torment. They would die slowly and painfully, and they would know their executioner and *why* they were dying. He enjoyed going over different brutal ways to snuff out their lives with the most pain. From the moment he awakened each morning until he fell into restless sleep at night, thoughts of the most satisfying ways to kill them gnawed at his brain.

During his first week at the cabin, his days had become routine. From daybreak to that fitful nighttime sleep that he was becoming accustomed to, his mind reeled with thoughts of revenge. He tried to focus on his main objective, sorting out all that didn't fit with his purpose in life—with his final mission in combat.

After several cups of coffee and a light breakfast, he conditioned his body. Slowly at first with isometric exercises, geared to stretch every tendon, every muscle. Then he switched to vigorous calisthenics and after working up a heavy sweat he jogged through the woods. At first the running was painful because of his healing wounds and his overall poor condition. But he thrived on the pain. It kept his anger festering. He fed on it. He could see the smirks on the faces of his quarry turning to fear. *Especially the big redhead.* His suffering would have to be the worst—even more than what he had made Marna suffer—a lot more.

Each day Spence ran farther and pushed himself harder. He soon regained his old running prowess. He could feel the difference in his lungs. It helped to envision the redhead, his mouth slobbering in horror, a few yards in front of him, running for his life.

Spence remembered the training he had received in the Special Forces. He could hear his former sergeant barking commands, and he responded with even more exuberance than he had back then when he was young. Before the third week was out, he logged ten miles or better each day—effortlessly.

Returning to his cabin after his jaunts, he drank a glass or two of water and rested for a while. Then, before he cooled down, he paced himself through the obstacle course he had set up. In some ways, it proved more rigorous than the one in boot camp, and his included opportunities to hone his martial art skills along the way. He had fashioned mock adversaries out of sticks and old clothes. They all seemed to look like the big redhead. He punished them unmercifully as he raced through the training field, confident he could kill any man in his path. And kill he would; it was just a matter of time. Being anxious for blood was not enough, he needed to prepare himself—in both body and mind for combat. He had learned from his past sorrowful mistakes. *This time there would be no mistakes.*

*   *   *   *

"What are ya doin', Rafe? Cut it out, will ya? Gimme that blanket!" Joe Johnson whined, as he squirmed on the top bunk. He rubbed his eyes, trying to snuggle into the warmth of the covers that had been snatched away from him.

"Get outta bed or we'll leave without ya. I got my ass chewed for being late yesterday," Rafe snarled at his brother. "And it was your fault then too."

"Big deal. Just go. I'll hitch a ride—or walk."

"Okay! Suit yourself. But I'm tired of this shit. You know Uncle Louie didn't have to give us a job or a place to live."

"*Some job*! Working our asses off, cutting down trees for piss-poor wages. How long we gonna stay in these woods? I'm starting to feel like an animal." Joe rubbed his arms vigorously to get rid of the chill. He managed to sit up on the edge of the bunk, his legs dangling over the side.

"Aw, come on, Joe, hop to it," Jake Green said. "All you need is a little pussy. We've been without for too long now. Tonight we're gonna hit town and hunt some till we get it—one way or another, huh, Rafe?"

"Yeah, that's what Friday nights are for," Rafe said, "drinking beer and fuckin'. But that's *after work*, so hurry it up. We'll wait ten minutes in the truck and that's all."

Joe scowled at them as they left the cabin. His body shivering, he slid from the bed and walked over to the fireplace. No wonder he was freezing. Only glowing embers remained in the hearth, and very little heat radiated from them. Usually he awakened to a crackling fire that took the nighttime chill off the cabin. Maybe his brother was simply teaching him to get up earlier. And maybe it was working, because he hustled into his jeans quicker than usual.

Hearing the engine of the beat up Chevy truck roar to life, Joe hurried out the cabin door, a cup of coffee in his hand. Rafe had gunned down the lane a distance of about half a city block, fully intending to leave him. But seeing in his rearview mirror that Joe had stepped outside, he braked the truck to a shuddering halt and waited for him to climb into the cab.

Buzzing power saws droned throughout the forest like a horde of angry, giant hornets whose nest had been disturbed. The cry of "timber-r-r" rose frequently above the din.

Sweat dripping from his forehead, Joe shut off his saw long enough to wipe his eyes with the back of his hand. He glanced at his watch one more time. Still an hour to 10:00 o'clock break. The day sure dragged. Unusually slow for a Friday with a paycheck and a night on the town to look forward to. Fridays were supposed to go fast. At least they had always seemed to go fast when he was back in high school, planning his weekends.

Yanking the starter cord on his saw, he continued to cut away the branches from the huge pine tree he had felled. *He had been out of high school five years.* And where was he? A fly-by-night lumberjack in Canada without hopes of a promotion. He detested the job even though he knew it would be only temporary. Drifting with Rafe across the states had given him all kinds of job experience. Pouring cement in Texas, driving a truck in Arizona, landscaping in California. Some jobs he liked better than others. But none of them led anywhere. He and his brother were always moving on. Usually one jump ahead of the law. And for a few years he had enjoyed the excitement of seeing new places and meeting new people, but somehow that part of it was getting old. He longed for something constant in his life—*something besides trouble.*

He remembered how it had been in high school. He and his buddies always thought of fun things. Games. Parties. *And the girls.* He wondered if some of the ones he had dated ever married—especially Jan Wagner. They had been getting along pretty well in their senior year. That was until she had mentioned marriage after graduation. He had been stunned by the thought. He had planned to go to college. She had taken it rather hard when he suggested that they were getting *too close*—that maybe they should date other people. *And what about college?* Several teachers had convinced him that he would do well by continuing his education. One had even said that with his aptitude for math and science the whole world was open to him. Another teacher had said, "Go to a computer school; that's the future. A lot of money in it. You won't be sorry."

Maybe if Rafe had gone to college on a football scholarship things would be different in both their lives. *He knew all too well why Rafe didn't go.* The college scouts were certainly interested in him. He had broken the school's all-time rushing record at fullback with half the season to go yet. But he had gotten a cheerleader pregnant, and her parents tried to pressure him into marriage. Rafe convinced them he was not marriage material. He started drinking lots of beer and getting into fights. One night he had gotten picked up for drunken driving, and because he fought with the police, he had to stay in jail for a whole weekend. He had been dismissed from the football team with three important games still to be played. And without football in his life, he had soured on school completely and dropped out three months before graduation. So that had ended Rafe's prospects for college.

But why hadn't *he* attended college? He had planned to. But what went wrong? He remembered the night Rafe had told him that he was getting out of their hometown—in fact, getting out of state. And did he want to join him? They would make some big money, he had said. He was already making more money on construction than the highest paid teacher in their school. So why go to college?

"Ya can't afford to go next year anyway," Rafe said. "Work a year and save your money. You can always go to college later if you want."

Reluctantly, he had agreed. *Now five years later* he was still broke and thoughts of college had all but disappeared. It wasn't only the money. He was a wanted man now. Barroom brawls and robbery were bad enough. But tack on rape and murder raps, and he wasn't sure he had a future. How far did brotherly love go anyway? Rafe had always seemed to care about him, especially when they were younger. Even though the school Joe attended was on the rough side, no one ever messed with him because that guy knew he'd have to answer to Rafe. But that was then.

Sure he had raped that girl on the island, but she didn't deserve to be murdered. Nor did any of the others. They were the kind of girls he would have been dating if he had gone to college. The nightmares because of that island rampage still remained. Rafe had not gone into details. He had merely said, "We wasted 'em. All of 'em, including that hero we fought with back in Ely."

What would happen to him if they were caught? He'd be judged an accomplice even though he had tried to talk them out of killing the girls. Life in prison or maybe the chair. He didn't know the laws of Minnesota concerning murder. Either way it was too high of a price to pay for family ties. And Rafe shouldn't have gotten him involved. But the fact remained—*he was involved*. Nothing could change that now.

After stripping the tree of all of its branches and cutting it into sections, he hooked chains to each log. Rafe or one of the other 'dozer men would come along and drag them down to the loading area where they would be hoisted onto trucks. At break, he found Rafe and Jake plotting their night's activities.

"Hey, little brother, we heard of just the place to start our weekend," Rafe said, as he sat on the ground, resting against a log. "It's called Pine Ridge Lodge. They've got a Happy Hour that includes all kinds of free chow. Guys go there just to eat supper. And later on they got dancing, but more important—the place is always loaded with love-starved chicks. They always outnumber the guys it seems. How about that?"

"One place is as good as another, I guess," Joe said, half-heartedly.

"Whatdya mean, *I guess*. We're gonna have a ball. Ain't that right, Jake?"

"Count on it, man," Jake said. "And it's about time. My pecker needs some practice 'cuz it's forgetting what it's for."

Joe passed his break time in relative quiet. The other two jawed excitedly about what they were going to do to satisfy themselves that evening.

Back at work, alone with his thoughts once again, Joe pondered over their conversation. God help the women they would meet that night. Hadn't they had enough sex to last a lifetime. It seemed to him their lives hadn't changed one bit. He wasn't sure that he could *get it up anymore himself*—after what had happened on the island. But it would be easier to go along with them—at least one more time. But something had to change soon. His nerves were getting frazzled living life on the wild side.

CHAPTER 16

▼

Spencer awakened earlier than usual. He wanted to make his last day of training especially productive. He would test himself to the maximum, reassuring himself that he was ready, physically and mentally. He would not try to fool himself, pretending to be fit if he were not, because this mission was too important. If he felt that he needed more time for any phase of his conditioning then he would take it—as simple as that. No hurry. Even though he found that he was growing more anxious with each passing day. He had been at Ducky's cabin for five weeks. The bullet wounds in his chest and head were healing nicely—better than he had expected them to. He could jog ten miles without the painful exhaustion he suffered that first week. He could run through his obstacle course with a vigor he had not felt in years.

As he slipped into his sweats, he knew he was ready for phase two of his seek-and-destroy mission. The day's activities would convince him—of that he was certain.

His mind reeled as he swung into his isometric exercises. He would leave Ely at 6:00 in the morning. Knowing that taking the same route would produce grim memories, he, nevertheless, opted to go that way. He would reconstruct the entire tragedy and concentrate on his mistakes so that he would not repeat them. He would pick up the scent of fear and terror and allow his psyche to absorb it—making it work for him. His former weakness would become his strength. Vengeance would prevail over any thoughts of mercy—driving him onward to exterminate his enemies.

Having completed his daily regimen in record time, Spence leaned against a birch tree, sweat dripping from his body. He felt exhilaration as he looked to the North. "I'm coming, you bastards," he said out loud. "Enjoy yourselves while you still can."

At 3:30 in the afternoon, Spence wheeled the Ford pickup to a screeching halt in front of the Last Chance Saloon. He had promised Ducky that he'd spend a few hours with him before his departure. Still feeling exuberant from his morning work-out, Spence jauntily stepped into the tavern. He couldn't help comparing the quiet of the place to the raucous shouting he had waltzed in on the last time he had been there. He spotted Ducky wiping the far end of the bar with a towel. "Hey, old timer, can a guy get a drink in here or do I hafta go next door?" he chided.

Recognizing his voice, Ducky wheeled around. "Don't *old timer me*, or you'll have to go to the next town to get a drink."

"The day you quit being so ornery is the day they'll bury you," Spence laughed.

"My customers wouldn't like it if I started treatin' 'em nice."

"Try it once," a man chipped in from across the bar.

"No sass out of you, Frederick, or you'll be spending your afternoons down at the drugstore eating ice cream," Ducky growled, as reached for an empty mug.

"Promise me you'll never change," Spence said, as he straddled a bar stool.

"Don't worry," Ducky said, slamming the foaming beer down on the bar in front of him. "I came into the world crotchety, and I intend to go out that way."

"I'd bet money on it," Spence said.

"So you're pulling out in the morning, huh?"

"Yeah, the time has come for me to get a move on."

Waiting for the tune on the jukebox to kick in, Ducky said quietly, "Sheriff Grabow's been asking about you. Wondering what you've been up to."

"What did you tell him?"

"Nothing much. Said ya was resting up at my place cuz he already knew you was there. Then I told him you'd probably do a little fishing like ya planned to do before—before all this happened."

"And what did he say?"

"He said that sounded reasonable enough, but somehow he had the feeling that you was holding out on him. Like you knew something you wasn't telling him."

"Oh, he did, did he," Spence said, sipping his beer.

"Spence, it tain't none of my business, but I know ya got plans. And, well—ah—I just want to say that I hope you get those cocksuckers and cut off their balls. Bring 'em back in a sack, and I'll fry 'em on the griddle and feed 'em to the dogs—or maybe one of my customers."

"Whew," Spence said, wiping his brow. "I'll see what I can do, but I don't want the law on my tail. Leastways—not till I finish what needs to be done."

"Well, they sure ain't gonna find out from me what you're up to. I've seen too many bad'uns weasel out of their crimes. They get a light jail sentence, and they're back on the streets doing business as usual before their victims even get used to them being gone."

"You're right, Ducky. I've seen that happen once too often. Well, it's not going to happen this time. You can count on that."

"Be careful," Ducky said, giving Spence a thumbs up gesture. "I wanna see you again, and I don't wanna see your mug behind bars—or as the centerpiece in a casket."

"Don't worry, I'm planning on doing it *right* this time around," Spence said.

The tavern slowly filled up during the Happy Hour that lasted from 4:00 to 6:00. Two-fers were the main attraction, but the cheese and crackers Ducky set out along the bar seemed to go over well too.

Spence stayed until 8:00, nursing his drinks and eating a light supper. He didn't want to be sluggish in the morning.

"Good-bye, Ducky," he said, heading for the door.

"See ya around." Ducky waved his hand and smiled.

By 5:00 a.m., Spence had dressed, eaten breakfast, and carried his two packs to the truck. Ducky had said he could take the Ford to his point of departure and leave it there till he got back out of the Boundary Waters. He had made arrangements with Matt Blake for another canoe, and again it would be his for as long as he needed it.

As he drove along Fernberg Road, Spence was conscious of the clear, blue August sky and the warm day shaping up. He planned to make it to Lake Alice by noon of his second day out. He would pick up his rifle and other supplies that he had left on the northern shore, and that meant he would pass by the site of the grim murders. He knew he would beach his canoe and check out the island, not really hoping to find any clues to the murderers' exact destination—but the memories of that grisly scene would rekindle his deep hatred for his enemies. And that's where he would pick up their trail—in the proper mood.

*   *   *   *

By 8:00 p.m., a thin bluish haze of smoke had settled over the spacious barroom of the Pine Ridge Lodge. People, mostly in their early twenties, jammed the place, but a good smattering of the over-thirty crowd popped up throughout the night, too. People waited in line outside the doors, anxious for someone to leave so they could join in the noisy revelry inside. The dance floor was filled to capacity as each new song blared from the stereo system.

Rafe nodded toward two women, stepping it off not far from the bar where he sat sideways on his stool. "See! What did I tell you, Joe. Some kind of meat market, huh?"

"Yeah, there sure are some nice looking girls. No doubt about that," Joe said. He found himself getting into the party mood despite his earlier intentions to drink moderately for the evening. The long day's work in the hot sun had produced a thirst he couldn't seem to quench—no matter how much beer he drank.

"There's gotta be some of these girls that like fuckin' as much as we do," Jake laughed.

"Don't worry about that none," Rafe said. "But it's too early to tell which ones will oblige us. Gotta wait till later when they're a little juiced up and they start gettin' sociable."

"Yeah, but it ain't too early to start narrowing down the odds," Jake countered.

The three of them continued drinking beer and checking out the scenery. Joe kept eyeing a brunette on the opposite side of the horseshoe-shaped bar. And it appeared that she was enjoying his stares. Her two girl friends seemed oblivious to the amount of friendly signals she was sending his way. Her eyes met repeatedly with Joe's, and he finally gave her a wide-open smile and gestured toward her in a kind of salute with his beer glass. She laughed and returned his "hello." That was enough for him to make his move. Beer in hand, he picked his way through the noisy crowd to her side of the bar.

"Hi," Joe said, his voice barely cutting through the din.

"Hello, Yank," the girl said with an obvious French accent.

"How do you know I'm from the States?" he asked.

"Well, I know you're not from Japan," she giggled. "Besides, I can tell Yanks a mile off. A certain way they carry themselves. And a certain way they look at girls."

"Is that right? Let me buy you a drink, and you can tell me *why* I stand out in such a crowd."

"Sure. I'll have another beer."

He signaled the bartender for two draws. Her friends paused in their conversation just long enough to acknowledge his presence with friendly nods and then squeezed closer together to make room for him at the bar.

Glancing across the room, Joe was glad that Rafe and Jake were not gawking at him.

When the beers arrived, the girl took hers and made a toast. "Here's to you, Yank. Isn't that the way you do it down there?"

"Yeah, something like that. Ever been to the States?"

"Several times. I've got relatives in South Dakota in a little town called Tindel. Ever hear of it?"

"Nope. Well, I've heard of South Dakota," he quipped.

"Ha! Ha!" she laughed, her soft brown eyes sparkling.

"Now, how is it you can tell a Yank from a Canuck?" he asked.

"You look over-confident. And you stare right through a girl. Your body language is completely different. I don't know how to explain it exactly. It's just something I sense. I haven't been wrong yet."

"Meet a lot of men, ah—erYanks, I mean?"

"Some. Mostly on Friday nights—like now."

Not sure where all this chitchat was leading, Joe asked her to dance.

"Sure," she said. "Why not?"

Getting to the dance floor was no easy task. The crowd was getting more *sociable* as Rafe called it. People were screaming to be heard. Waitresses were bumping into one another, trying to deliver drinks fast enough.

By the time Joe and the girl reached the dancing area, the music had changed from rousing fast pieces to slow, seductive French songs. Joe didn't mind. The thought of holding this good-looking woman close excited him.

"What's your name?" he asked, as they shuffled along, barely able to move in the crowd.

"Jacylyn Renoux. Jackie for short. Let me guess yours. You look like ah—ah—a Robert."

"Close! My name is Joe Johnson," he said, holding her a little tighter. It felt good being so close to an attractive, friendly woman. This was the way it was supposed to be. *Only—only what?* He wondered what she'd do now if she realized that she was dancing with a rapist. But any feelings of guilt that were creeping in were overshadowed by the tremendous high he was enjoying—partly as a result of the beer and partly because of her warm body.

People nearby stopped dancing and stared toward the bar. There was a commotion of some kind. Glancing over Jackie's shoulder, Joe scowled. Three of the tavern's bouncers were closing in on Rafe.

"Excuse me a minute, Jackie. That's my brother." Joe pushed his way through the crowd toward Rafe.

"I was only having a little fun, guys," Rafe said. "Most girls *I know* liked to be pinched in the ass."

"Obviously, monsieur," one of the men said curtly, "this one does not. So if you'll please follow me."

"Wait a minute," Rafe balked. "I'm not ready to leave yet. I want to dance a little and drink a little. Shit! I pinched seven or eight girls tonight. This bitch is the only one who objected."

Her boyfriend had happened to notice her obvious jump, when Rafe had pinched her, and, after conversing with her, he had returned to confront Rafe. Rafe had responded by giving the man a shove, knocking him backwards into a waitress who spilled her tray of drinks. The bouncers had hurried toward the big redheaded man like sharks to bloody meat.

"Jesus, Rafe, cool it." Joe screamed. "Let's get out of here. *Now!*"

Rafe was about to protest, but Jake calmed him by saying, "Joe's right. It's time to head for another bar."

They zigzagged through the crowd with one of the doormen in the lead and two following close at their heels. Joe glanced longingly back at Jackie who blew him a kiss. *Nothing was ever going to change in his life, as long as he stayed with Rafe.*

CHAPTER 17

▼

Rounding a bend in the narrow stream that fed into Lake Alice, Spence looked across the wide expanse of water to the *island of death*. The sandy beach sparkled in the mid morning sun. He remembered how choppy the waters had been when he had ventured two months before across the lake with the girls. Today the water remained calm as he paddled effortlessly toward the far shore. He had arrived two hours ahead of schedule, mainly because he had not encountered many canoeists at the portages. The few people he had come across didn't delay him in the least. He had merely nodded at them and continued on his way. He had had no desire to carry on idle talk. For one reason, his vengeful mood had dictated a controlled profile, and also he had purposely decided to remain as inconspicuous as possible in his travels. He didn't want anyone to be able to identify him later on, *just in case* he had to account for his whereabouts to the law. But then why should he have to? If things went according to plan, three men would simply disappear from the face of the earth. The police couldn't find them *now*. Spence would merely see to it that their absence remained permanent.

Relieved to see no one camping on the island, Spence beached his canoe. There was no need to unpack since he only planned to stay there a few minutes. He had not looked forward to this moment, knowing he would have to force himself to endure the memories of the massacre.

Approaching the campsite, Spence noticed how well the police and the rangers had groomed the island. If he had not experienced near death in the same area, he would only view it for what it was supposed to be—a wilderness paradise. Nothing remained to indicate the slaughter that had taken place there.

Birds chirped friendly songs, and ground squirrels scurried from hole to hole around the perimeter of the campsite, hopeful that this new visitor would provide them with scraps of food. The sun warmed Spence's back as he sat at the table, his elbows propped on the hard surface, his hands covering his face. His mind reeled over the grisly scenes of his last trip to that island. The more he thought about them, the more horrid they became. The gruesome visions of a naked man butchering naked women with a bloody knife flashed through his mind like some triple x-rated horror film. *And isn't that what the man named Jake had pretended?* To make a film with them as the principals—a Snuff film—he had called it.

Spence would see that there was a sequel—more bloody than the first one. He retched as bile flooded to his throat and mouth, the acid burning his insides. That internal reflex action probably kept him from blacking out from the horrible thoughts that ran wildly through his mind. Even in his misery, as he stumbled toward the lake for a drink of water to douse the fire enflaming his innards, he felt some relief to know that he had not lost consciousness. That was a weakness he could not very well afford, if he was to stay on top of things and be in complete control. His blackouts as a result of reliving torture scenes from Vietnam had caused him momentary embarrassment in the past, but fading away on *this* mission could cost him his life.

Dipping his cup into the clear water, he gargled first and spit onto the shore. Then he swallowed several mouthfuls of the cool water washing the bitter taste back down to the depths of his stomach. Splashing water on his face and hair made him feel a little better.

This was the spot where the trail began. His foot resting on the prow of his canoe, Spence looked to the North. He knew of several ways to sneak into Canada without being noticed by border officials. Maybe with a little luck, he would pick the same one that his enemies had taken. But even if he didn't, it didn't matter. Once he got to Canada he would ferret them out, if he had to travel to every city in every province to do it. Somebody would remember those guys. Three Americans. One of them a tall hulk of a man with red hair. He would find them all right. It was just a matter of time.

Spence pushed away from the shore and paddled north to the campsite where he had stashed most of his equipment, including his rifle, just before he had tried to rescue the girls. He hoped everything would still be there, but if it wasn't, he wouldn't panic, for he had brought enough new supplies to survive his trek through the wilds.

The August sun felt good on his body, as he made long, even strokes with his paddle. Loons diving for fish didn't seem to be distracted as his canoe knifed through their feeding area. His conditioning had paid dividends already, his body performing like a well-oiled machine. He had realized his increased stamina in some of the longer portages. Even with his canoe on his shoulders, he was able to maintain a steady gait. Now he relished the thought that each time he pulled back his paddle, he was a little closer to his enemies.

Within the hour, he approached the familiar campsite at the northern end of Lake Alice. He landed on a large flat rock that extended from the shore out into the lake just below water level. Having pulled his canoe ashore far enough so it wouldn't float away, Spence walked toward several huge boulders. In his haste to get to the island where the girls had been, he had not hidden his equipment as carefully as he might have, but, at least he protected it from the elements. Everything remained intact. No one had stumbled onto his belongings, or if they had, they left them alone.

He checked his rifle first, putting the pieces together, and sighting through the scope at a distant pine tree. Then he carefully broke the weapon down again and inserted it into his pack. The rest of his equipment was in order too. He had gambled that his tent would still be there so he wouldn't wind up with two. He had reasoned back in Ely that he could survive without the comforts of a tent if need be, but it was still in its pack.

Not wanting to waste time building a fire, Spence ate two peanut butter sandwiches and washed them down with two cups of cool water. He would catch some fish later on in the day and fry them for supper whenever he decided to camp for the night.

Setting out once again, Spence headed up a narrow channel linking Lake Alice with Cacabic Lake. There he would have to undertake a 238 rod portage which would involve considerable inconvenience, but it was a short cut to Lake Thomas where he hoped to camp for the night. It was not the quickest way to Canadian border, but it was more remote and offered fewer chances of bumping into Canadian Customs' officials. He pondered whether or not his adversaries would be smart enough to take the same route or take an easier one that allowed for more canoeing and fewer portages, but would have heavier risks of being stopped by officials. He hoped they wouldn't be caught before he found them. Prison was too good for those animals—much too good! He knew exactly what they needed! *And after he was through with them, they would never need anything ever again!*

*   *   *   *

The three men staggered toward their truck.

"I'd like to stay around and kick ass," Rafe fumed, glancing back toward the doorway where one of the bouncers stared at them, his arms folded in front of him.

"Jesus, Rafe!" Joe wailed. "Haven't we got enough trouble? We're supposed to be coolin' it! *Remember?*"

"Aw, fuck it," Rafe slurred. "Take it as it comes."

"Yeah. I hear ya! Might as well get fitted for prison blues because *that's what's coming next*. Right?" Joe screamed, pounding his fist into the truck door.

"Hey, you guys!" Jake said. "We're out to fuck some cunt tonight. Now let's just go to another bar and have a good time. I'm getting tired of you two fighting. Maybe you oughtta just slug it out and be done with it."

"Maybe you oughtta keep your mouth shut, or maybe you want a piece of me!" Rafe snarled.

"That time might be comin' 'cuz I'm gettin' sick of you two jawing at one another." Jake looked menacingly at Rafe.

"That's great, fuckin' great! Why don't we just kill one another and be done with it." Joe glared at Jake.

"Easy, little brother, easy. You're not starting to crack on us, are you? We're in this together whether we like it or not."

"Don't count me in on the murders. I had nothing to do with that. *And keep that straight!*" Joe had never actually stated verbally what he had been thinking about the killing, and he realized it was a mistake to have mentioned it now.

"Wouldn't be planning to turn us in would you, Joe?" Rafe asked, lowering his voice.

"I don't know what I want to do. But I can't stand this shit anymore. I think maybe we oughtta split up."

"Oh, you do, huh? Well, let me tell you something. We ain't separatin'. We stay together, no matter what! You got that?"

"For the time being that's *all* I got," Joe said, "but I'm not living like this forever; I'll tell you that."

"Okay! Okay! But let's get the hell out of here," Rafe insisted.

After they piled into the truck, Rafe gunned out of the parking lot. As they passed the lodge, he yelled, "Fuck you," and gave the man in the doorway the finger.

*   *   *   *

Spence sat looking at the fire, mesmerized. Why was it that fires have such hypnotic affects on people? Whatever the reasons, a fire provided good company for a man alone. But more often than not, a campfire would conjure up thoughts of nighttime in Vietnam, those few instances when they were allowed to have a fire—then only in what had been declared a *"safe area."* Spence chuckled to himself. What part of Vietnam had been safe? He had seen guys blown to bits while eating in Saigon restaurants.

Sometimes a campfire reminded him of his fishing and hunting expeditions he had taken with his father. Thoughts of those good times would relax him, making him sleepy.

Sparks flaring up when he put another log on the fire, Spence realized that his thoughts tonight centered on the time he had built a huge fire on the beach for the girls. Their friendly banter. And his walk with Marna along the shore. And then he would drift into a seething rage, thinking of their murderers alive and well somewhere in Canada, and him getting closer to them each day. He wondered if they knew he was stalking them. Did they even know that he was alive? Would they have read about their butcher job in the papers? The media had given all the gory details they could squeeze out of the police. They certainly didn't get much information from him. He remembered how angry the reporters got when he simply refused to satisfy their curiosity. Would the murderers even be concerned with what they had done? Were they holing up in some backwoods just biding their time? Or were they afraid they would be caught? He hoped they were living in fear. That thought suited him best.

When his fire reduced itself to hot glowing coals, Spence stepped into his tent and crawled into his sleeping bag. He forced himself to concentrate on sleep, so he would be rested for another long day of canoeing.

During the night, the growling of a black bear lumbering through his camp, awakened him. He remained tense as the bear foraged for food even brushing the tent in his search. Spence gripped his .45, knowing that if the bear entered his tent he would shoot him in the head. He didn't come all this way to be mauled by a bear. Not finding any food, the bear "woofed" and then retreated to the woods. When Spence was satisfied that he was gone for good, he rolled over and managed to sleep the rest of the night.

By 5:30, Spence sat up. He felt rested and ready for the day, thankful that the bear hadn't ruined an otherwise good night's sleep. After splashing water from the lake on his face to perk himself up, he built a small fire. He made coffee and cooked pancakes. Satisfying his hunger, he broke camp and set out due north once again, hoping to reach the end of Lake Thomas late in the afternoon. There, a short 15-rod portage would get him to Gerund Lake which he could cross in about twenty minutes. A 90-rod portage would connect him with Wisini Lake where he planned to camp for the night.

*   *   *   *

The four men eyed the rowboat tied to the makeshift dock.

"Think it'll hold us?" Rafe asked.

"Well, it would've yesterday, but after all that beer you guys drank last night, I'm not so sure," Uncle Louie laughed.

"Very funny," Rafe said.

"It's pretty late for fishing. Will they be biting?" Joe asked, half hoping they would cancel out, and he could go back to bed and sleep off his hangover.

"I told you to come at 7:00 a.m., but you're three hours late. And that doesn't really surprise me. But don't worry. The fish in this lake are always hungry. You'll see."

Rafe manned the oars after all of them got seated. He pulled with all his might, but the boat stayed close to the dock.

"C'mon, Rafe, did you lose it all on that whore last night?" Jake chided. "We're not moving yet."

Rafe grew angry, his face turning redder by the minute. He dragged the oars through the water again. Still no movement. "What the fuck is goin' on? This thing anchored?" he asked.

"Oh, I forgot to mention," Louie said. "This boat only goes backwards for some reason. Never could figure it out."

"You're kidding," Rafe snarled, thinking Louie was joking.

"No, I'm not! Turn it around and see for yourself."

Rafe, lifted one oar out of its lock and pushed hard against the dock. The boat spun around with the prow pointing toward shore. With his back to the open water, Rafe pulled hard on the oars, and the boat moved away easily from the dock. "I'll be damned. Got yourself a tricky boat here."

Joe was not the least bit amused. His head pounded and his throat felt dry. It had been 4:00 a.m. when they had arrived at the cabin—all of them ornery. Rafe and Jake never did find any "sociable" girls. They had to settle for a two-bit whore in a back room at one of the taverns they wandered into. He had kept drinking beer, trying to forget what was really on his mind—*getting far away from the other two*, at least for a while so he could think things out.

He certainly had no intentions of going fishing. He didn't even like to fish. But here he was in the rowboat bound for the middle of Lake Blue. Despite his agony, he was still able to appreciate the beauty of the kidney-shaped lake, its water ocean blue against a thick forest of pine trees.

"Pull in by that stick," Louie commanded, as they approached the bend in the middle of the lake. "And drop anchor."

Rafe followed instructions. He and Jake then prepared their rod-and-reels.

"Mighty fancy equipment you got there," Louie said, his eyes beaming.

"Where's your pole, Louie?" Rafe asked.

"Right here in my pocket," he said, pulling a coiled rope out of a front pocket of his jeans. A large silver hook, minus a barb, dangled from the end of the rope. He whirled the rope about his head several times and then flung the hook out into the water. Letting it sink for a few seconds, Louie hauled in the rope, hand over hand.

A huge walleye struck the hook when it was about five feet from the boat. Louie pulled in the rope faster than before—giving it a jerk, as the fish got within a foot of the boat. The fish flopped into the boat, its mouth open, displaying rows of sharp teeth.

"Jesus," Rafe said, "that was quick! You don't mess around, do you, Louie?"

"Can't afford to. I don't have time to fish for sport. Up here we live on fish year round." He had already whipped his hook back into the water. Again, as he hauled it in, another walleye, the same size as the last one, hit the silver hook. Louie had four fish in the boat before Jake and Rafe attached their lures and prepared to cast.

"And to think I was about to go swimming in that water," Joe said. "But not anymore. Look at the teeth on those suckers, and they're so goddamned hungry."

The others laughed. By 2:00 in the afternoon, they had caught forty fish in all. The boat was so full that some actually flipped over the side back into the water till Jake spread a net over them.

While they docked the boat, Louie's wife and daughter stood on the shore cheering their catch, even though they knew they'd spend the rest of the day cleaning and preparing the fish to be smoked.

*   *   *   *

Spence paddled away from shore, relieved that the long portage was over. He would be entering Lake Wisini in plenty of time before darkness set in.

CHAPTER 18

▼

Joe spent Sunday in a foul mood. He had lain awake most of Saturday night trying to plan his future—what he could make of it anyway. There were too many negative circumstances in his life that made him hate to face each new day. Hiding from the law in the backwoods with two murderers—one of them his own brother, working at a job that he detested, and knowing that he and Rafe were not as close as they used to be—all these things gnawed at him. He needed time on his own to think.

If only he had someone he could share his inner feelings with. What was that woman's name he had met in the bar? Jackie? He remembered how nice it had been holding her close. That's what he longed for—female companionship. Someone who really cared how he felt inside. It had been a long time since he had been intimate with anyone.

He had traveled across the country going from job to job, hoping he would find a place to settle down—a place where he would be happy to live. Each time he would start feeling comfortable, Rafe would get restless *or* get into trouble *or* both. Then they would depart quickly to follow another dream. There had been good times, but during the last two years, Joe had felt something eating away at him. The bad times were becoming too frequent. The last straw was the murder of those five people.

Wishing it away didn't ease his mind any. The thought of his involvement hung like a millstone around his neck.

Tossing and turning in his bed, he had decided that he would make his break to freedom and sanity. After all, what did he owe Rafe that he had not already paid him by living in misery as a hunted criminal.

He knew it would not be easy to escape, especially since he had blurted out his feelings on Friday night. Rafe had been eyeing him suspiciously ever since. He had been adamant in his decision that the three of them stick together. Rafe would never forgive him if he bolted and separated from him. *And a part of him still cared what Rafe thought about him.* Another part of him feared what Rafe might do in reprisal, if he ever caught up with him again. But his overwhelming desire to live a decent, carefree life dominated his thoughts—no matter what the consequences. He had to get away—to be alone for a while. Winnipeg would be a big enough city in which to lose himself, get a good paying job, and start saving for a trip back to the states. And then maybe look up some old friends, maybe buy a car and enjoy life for a change. But he would have to be careful. He didn't want Rafe to realize what his intentions were till it was too late. *Till he was safe.*

He had planned to feign sickness all day Sunday so that on Monday it would seem reasonable if he didn't go to work. And when Rafe and Jake took off in the truck he would shag it to the highway and hitch a ride northwest to Winnipeg. Maybe even take a bus part of the way if need be. He had saved a few bucks for just such an emergency.

Sunday passed by very slowly. Joe stayed in bed most of the morning, groaning and pretending to be sick.

"What's the matter with you?" Rafe asked. "Still got a hangover from Friday?"

"No, it must be something I ate or maybe it's the flu, but I don't feel with a shit," Joe said. He had gone to the outhouse at least five times and even forced himself to throw-up once, careful to let some of the vomit drip onto his T-shirt, making sure that he even smelled sick.

"Well, you're making me sick just looking at ya. Think maybe Jake and me will drive over to Louie's for a few hours. He's having some of the boys in to play cards. Will you be okay?"

"Yeah!"

"Lay off the booze and don't eat anything. You'll be fine by morning."

"Gees, I hope so," Joe said halfheartedly.

"Hey, don't beat your meat either," Jake said, hovering over the bed with a leer on his face. "It takes the tuck outta ya."

Joe responded by closing his eyes and turning on his side away from him.

As the truck roared down the lane, Joe peered out the window. "Fuck you, Rafe! And fuck you too, Jake," he muttered. "Tomorrow you can count me gone."

*   *   *   *

On Sunday at 5:00 a.m., Spence's internal alarm awakened him, but he was not in any hurry to jump up and start things rolling. He had put in a long, arduous day paddling on Saturday, and it was nearly nightfall when he had pulled into a campsite on the northern end of Wisini Lake.

He lay in his bedroll savoring the warmth and peace of the moment. His mind drifted back to the Sundays of his youth. He had been raised a Roman Catholic, so attending mass had been a matter of habit with him. It had been part of the ritual of the day. Most often he had gone to church with his foster parents, and afterward they would go out somewhere for brunch. Those had been good times in which he always told them about his plans for the upcoming week—what was going on at school—especially the sporting events. They had been his ardent fans and seldom missed any of his games whether at home or on the road. And he always felt proud when they were in the stands. He played extra hard when they were there—not because they had pushed sports on him so much, as the fact that he just wanted to show them how much he appreciated what they had done for him. They had been loving parents.

Somewhere between high school and college graduation, his attendance at Sunday mass on a regular basis had fallen off. He had adopted the attitude that God would love him whether he went to church or not, and so it became easier and easier to stay in bed on Sunday mornings, especially after Saturday nights on the town.

Vietnam had knocked any attempts at formal religion out of him. For a time he had even refused to believe that God existed. He had seen too much suffering and reasoned that God would not allow it to happen. But then there had been plenty of times when he faced imminent death that he relied on God for comfort. The old saying, "*No atheists in foxholes,*" had crossed his mind. And maybe none in the steamy jungles of Vietnam either. Then too, some of the guys had been so spaced out on drugs they didn't care about living or dying *or whether God existed or not.*

As he lay in his tent feeling the warmth of the sun, he vowed not to let religion get in the way of his vendetta. God would forgive him for what he must do. His conscience remained clear on that issue; *he wouldn't allow it to be otherwise.*

After drowsing for three-quarters of an hour in half asleep-half awake euphoria, Spence forced himself to get up and face the day. An 85-rod portage separated Lake Wisini from Lake Kekekabic. And after a day of steady paddling, he would be in a position to cross over to the South Arm of Knife Lake which connected to Knife Lake Proper—the boundary between the U.S.A. and Canada. If he didn't dally and didn't run into unforeseen difficulties, he would be in Canada by late Wednesday afternoon. And once there, he would purposely start making contact with people, hoping to pick up some clues that would lead him to the whereabouts of those butchers he longed to kill—*ever so slowly.*

*   *   *   *

By Monday morning, Joe had done so well pretending to be sick that when he struggled to get up for work, Rafe yelled at him and told him to stay in bed.

"We can get by without you for a day or two, little Brother. Just take it easy. There's some Chicken Noodle soup in the cupboard, if you feel up to eating later on." Rafe affectionately patted his shoulder.

"Thanks. I'll be okay," Joe said, his voice hoarse sounding.

"We'll pick you up some 7-up on the way home from work," Jake added, "but by then you'll probably be well enough for beer. Right?"

"Yeah, sure," Joe groaned.

Tensing as the truck's engine roared to life, Joe waited five minutes till he was sure that Rafe had gunned the Ford down the road out of sight. He jumped out of bed, grinning. They had fallen for his little ruse all right. Everything was going according to plan. He hurried into his clothes and grabbed his duffel bag from under the bottom bunk. He would travel light—packing only necessary clothing and a .45 pistol. After a week's work in Winnipeg, he could buy whatever else he needed.

*   *   *   *

"Where the hell is he?" Rafe growled, storming around the cabin like a caged wolf.

"How should I know?" Jake said. "Maybe he went for a walk or something. No reason to panic."

"Yeah, that's what you say. You know he's been acting strange lately. Check out in back."

Slamming the door, Jake circled the cabin. Not seeing Joe or any sign of him, he hurried to make his report.

"Nothing," he said.

"Wait a minute; there's a note." Rafe hurried to the fireplace. He read aloud: "Rafe, I know you'll be pissed off at me, but you'll get over it. I can't stand things as they are. I want to get on with my life. Everything's closing in on me—smothering me. I've got to get away on my own. Don't worry about me; I'll be okay. And I'll keep my mouth shut. Maybe we'll meet again someday under better circumstances."

"*Maybe we'll meet again someday*," Rafe repeated, mockingly. "That fucker! He can count on that! After all I've done for him ever since he was just a snot-nosed kid."

"Which way do ya think he went?" Jake asked.

"I dunno, but I'll tell you one thing. We're gonna find him. Can't have him running around the country, spilling his guts—brother or no brother. We gotta stay together till it's safe."

"What are we gonna do? It's a hell of a big world, and we gotta stay low."

"Well, it's too late to find him tonight. Tomorrow we'll check at work with the guys. Maybe he talked to one of them about a hiding place. And *just maybe* one of the truckers spotted him on the road hitching a ride. He can't get far on foot. Don't worry none. We'll find that little cocksucker, and he'll be sorry he made a run for it. I've been too easy on him, but that's gonna change."

*   *   *   *

Feeling exhilarated for having finally made his break to freedom, Joe walked briskly along Highway 17. He had avoided the familiar roads that he knew the loggers favored. He had not wanted any truckers innocently passing on information about him back at camp. Car after car passed him without slowing down. He had begun to wonder if he'd have to walk the entire distance to Winnipeg. After two hours of steady trekking, he managed to hitch a ride with a middle-aged man who was traveling to Dryden about forty miles away.

"Thanks," Joe said, after hopping into the front seat of the blue Cougar.

"Where are you heading?" the man asked, glancing toward him.

"I hope to make it to Kenora by nightfall."

"You're a Yank, aren't ya?"

"Yep!"

"What are you doing up this way?"

"I'm looking for work. Hope to find something in Winnipeg."

"Temporary or steady?"

"Steady, if I can land a job."

"You oughtta be able to find one. Got any skills?"

The guy sure was probing. At least it seemed that way to Joe. "Just odd jobs here and there, nothing special."

"Might try the meat packing plant there. Heard they were hiring seasonal workers. Might not be full-time, but it would give you some money till you found something more steady."

"I'll keep it in mind. Sounds like a good place to start looking any-way," Joe said, wondering if the real interrogation was about to start. "What do *you* do for a living?" he asked the man, switching the atten-tion away from himself.

"Oh, I sell insurance and dabble a little in real-estate. Both a little slow right now."

The two of them chatted all the way into Dryden. Joe weighed his words carefully, so as not to make the man the least bit suspicious. They had not even exchanged names, and that was fine as far as Joe was concerned.

He wondered how the man would react if he knew he had a .45 packed away in his duffel bag. It actually made him a little nervous to be carrying it. But he was traveling in a strange land, and he didn't want to take any shit from anybody. The gun offered him security.

"I'll drop you off at Meggie's. She runs a little cafe in town. She usu-ally knows everybody's business. Maybe she can steer you on to a ride to Kenora this afternoon. It's worth a try."

"Thanks again." Joe slammed the car door and waved goodbye. He felt good about his progress so far. He entered Meggie's café, hoping she would connect him with another ride.

*   *   *   *

"Well, well, if it isn't Sheriff Grabow," Ducky said, as he plunged two glasses into the water tank for rinsing. "What can I do for you?"

"Just a cup of coffee. I had a late breakfast, so I think I'll skip lunch," Grabow said, easing on to a stool. He was fifty-two years old, his hair completely gray, his face a mass of wrinkles—forming a perpetual scowl.

"Want it just like your women?" Ducky asked, wishing someone would create a new line for ordering coffee.

"You've got it. Hot and black."

"Don't you *wish*," Ducky chuckled, placing the steaming mug on the bar. "It's on me, long as ya don't come too often."

"Much obliged."

Ducky knew the sheriff well enough to guess that he wanted something. He could read it in his eyes.

"Spencer's been gone about a week now, right?" Grabow said, appreciative that they were alone.

"Yep. Now that you mention it. I kinda lose track of people's comin's and goin's."

"Funny thing about that guy. I still have a feeling that he never told us everything he knew about the murders—especially when it came to describing the ones that done it. Said he was unconscious or blindfolded and could only hear voices. Do you buy that, Ducky?"

"No reason not to. Why would he lie about something like that?"

"Just a hunch of mine, but if somebody tried to off *me* that way, and I had that fellow's training, I'd bet I'd like to get back at them before the law got 'em."

"Is that what you're hoping he'll do?"

"Nope! Nope! 'cuz then I'd be after *him* instead of *them*. And I know how close you two are."

"What's that supposed to mean?" Ducky growled.

"Nothing much. Only maybe you know something you ought to be telling me."

"Whenever I learn something that I think is your business, I'll call you. Then you won't have to come in here making crazy insinuations." Ducky's face turned a glowing red.

"Now, now, I don't want you to get all riled up. It's just that I got a feeling about Spence. I could see it in his eyes. That guy was fixing to do something mean. And by the way—some of your neighbors spotted him while he was at your cabin. One of 'em said it looked like he was in training for some kind of war."

"So the guy likes to stay in shape. That's no crime these days, is it, Sheriff?" Ducky lowered his eyes to Grabow's gut, bulging over his gun belt.

"Vietnam's over," Grabow retorted. "The laws of the jungle don't apply here. Just hope your friend knows that. Thanks for the coffee. Keep in touch." He left the tavern as Ducky cursed himself for allowing the man to rankle him. He did wonder where Spence was at this precise moment, and if he was in any danger.

*   *   *   *

Overhanging pine branches swished against the sides of Spence's canoe as he plodded along the unkempt narrow trail. He stared straight-ahead looking for the next canoe rest. His shoulders ached, and he longed for a fresh drink of water. On shorter portages, he usually made two trips—one with the canoe and another carrying his packs. But on this 85-rod portage, he had decided to lug it all at the same time and make use of the rest stops whenever he felt the urge. Rounding a bend in the path, Spence saw the canoe rest that he had been eagerly waiting for. He groaned audibly at the sight before him. A large tree, obviously struck by lightening in a recent storm, had fallen on the cross bar, smashing it to the ground. He paused momentarily, pondering if he could make the next one without stopping. Deciding he could not, he eased the canoe onto the ground. After rubbing his shoulders and stretching his arms, he sat down on the grass, resting his back on the prow of the canoe. He swigged from his canteen and then poured water over his head, letting it flood down over his face, refreshing him.

The sun, high in the sky directly above him, told him that it was noon. As long as he had stopped, he might as well eat a sandwich. Then once he made it to Lake Kekekabic, he could continue paddling till nightfall.

*   *   *   *

Joe wiped up the remains of the roast beef special on his plate with a slice of bread. The closest he had come to a home cooked meal in a long time. That Meggie was quite some cook. Not bad looking either though he reasoned she was pushing forty. He liked her smile, and her dark brown eyes seemed to bewitch him.

"Would you like some dessert?" she asked, her hip resting against the counter. "Our praline pie will send you into ecstasy."

"Sounds good," Joe said. "You convinced me—and could I have more coffee, please?"

"You're a new face," she said, sliding the pie plate up to him and refilling his coffee cup.

"Yeah, just passing through. Hope to make Kenora by evening. Know anyone headed that way?"

"Let me check. Hey, you guys," she screamed above the din. "Anybody going to Kenora this afternoon?"

Two men in a booth glanced her way. "Yeah, Meggie," one of them yelled out. "Right after lunch. Want to come along? We could take the scenic route."

"Don't tempt me," Meggie laughed. "This guy would like a ride."
She nodded toward Joe.

"Sure, why not," one of the men said, looking their way. "We'll be
hitting the road in a few minutes."

"Thanks," Joe said, looking up at Meggie, "I appreciate it." He'd
leave her an even bigger tip than he had intended.

"I aim to please," she said, winking at him.

CHAPTER 19

▼

Jake leaned his saw against a freshly cut tree and sat down on the ground beside it, using the log as a backrest. He pulled off his hard hat and tossed it to one side, not even looking to see where it landed. Opening his lunch pail, he unwrapped a summer sausage and cheese sandwich. Chomping in to it, he closed his eyes, resting. He had put in a hard morning. The work had not been more difficult than usual, but Louie had stormed around camp in a foul mood, berating any loggers in his path. His ranting made everyone uneasy, but they didn't work any faster. They merely kept up a steady pace and made sure Louie didn't spot them slowing down before the official break time.

Rafe approached Jake, his beard glistening fire-red in the sun.

"Find out anything?" Jake asked, rubbing sweat from his eyes.

"Not much," Rafe said, sitting down beside him. "It seems that he never talked much to the other guys. One man on his crew said he told Joe that someday he was gonna quit here and go to Winnipeg. He'd get a job making more pay and working a lot less, saving himself for chasing pussy every night. And it seems that Joe was interested at the time. But they never mentioned it again."

"Sounds like a good idea to me," Jake said, slurping his coffee. "Maybe *we* oughtta try it."

"If I knew for sure that's where Joe went, I'd head out after him right now."

"Would we quit here?"

"Nope. I like it here. Nobody asks many questions. It's a safe place to stay for the time being." Rafe said, tugging on his beard.

"What would you do then, if you found him?"

"I'd coldcock that little fucker, tie him up, and bring him back here in the truck. We could cover him up with a tarp. Nobody would even guess what we were hauling."

"Then what? Put a leash on him—a ball and chain or...."

"Don't get cute, Jake. After I beat the shit out of him a few times. He'd realize that what I say—goes."

"But ten to one, he'd take off again as soon as he was able. You know he's right about him not being in on the killings."

"You sound like he'd being doing the right thing," Rafe snarled.

"No! I don't like that asshole running around on his own any more than you do—maybe even less. You know he's the only one who could testify against us—if he ever started getting bright ideas."

"Joe wouldn't ever rat on us."

"Then let's just forget him—or maybe you know there's always that possibility. He could plea-bargain and get off free. And we'd be rottin' in prison. Just what *would* you do if you knew that he planned to fuck us over?"

"What are you getting at, Jake? You think I'd kill my own brother?"

"Maybe you'd have to."

"Yeah, that's right! And maybe I'd waste you too. Then *I'd be the only one* who knew what happened on that island."

"Or maybe I'd waste you first—or just maybe *I'd* make a deal to get a lesser charge," Jake fumed.

"Let's quit this kind of shit," Rafe growled, standing up. "It's time to get back to work." But he was uneasy with what had transpired between them. It gave him more to worry about than just finding his brother. It dawned on him that maybe Jake was an even bigger threat.

*   *   *   *

Darkness swallowed up the campsite on the small island at the eastern end of Lake Kekekabic where Spence worked intently to ignite a pile of twigs. He would build a fire and then fry the walleye he had caught trolling earlier. Gradually, he fed the fire larger sticks till it was time to set logs on the blaze.

As the fish sizzled in the skillet, Spence's ears perked up at the sound of a motor sputtering close by. He knew the source of that sound. While paddling toward shore in the twilight, he had observed a tent nestled among the trees on an island in the middle of the lake. For an instant, he had thought that he had gotten lucky. That he had actually stumbled on to his prey. But after checking out the campsite with his binoculars, he had seen only a man and woman busily fixing their supper. The motor coughed, then died. Putt-putted and killed again. After it quit a third time, Spence called out across the lake, "Need any help?"

"No, thanks," came the reply. So Spence returned to his campfire.

He had just eaten the last bit of fish when the two strangers approached his island, their motor working smoothly now. He assumed their motor was legal in this lake.

"Hello there," the man called as their canoe idled a few feet from shore.

"Hi, yourself," Spence yelled. "Care to join me?" He didn't need or want company, but maybe they could give him some information.

As they beached their canoe by the light of the fire, Spence observed that the woman was Indian, her long black hair spilling down over her shoulders.

After a lot of small talk, he asked them how long they had been camping on the lake.

"Been out here a month and two days," the man said. "Gotta be getting back to work pretty soon. Our vacation's about over."

"Where do you work?"

"I'm a maintenance man at a factory in Minneapolis. We come up here every other year just to get away from it all. Wouldn't mind living here year round. Would we, honey?"

"Not at all," his wife said, a pleasant smile on her plump face. "'Cept I don't think a tent would keep us warm enough in the winter."

"It gets cold all right," Spence said. "I've done some hunting up this way a few years back during the winter months. It's no place for amateurs. That's certain."

"What do you do for a living?" the man asked.

"I'm a school teacher," Spence said, not wishing to tell them any more than necessary. "I'm gonna try to surprise some buddies of mine. They came up this way on a fishing trip about a month back. Three of 'em. See anybody passing this way?" He couldn't very well tell them that he planned to kill his so-called "buddies."

"Don't see many people. That's why we come here. Almost complete solitude," the man said. "You're the first in a long time."

"One of them is a tall red-headed man," Spence continued. "And one...." His voice trailed off as the man's wife mumbled something in her Indian tongue. As near as Spence could make out, she had called the men, "bastards" or worse.

"Now that you mention it. Three guys did pass through here quite a while ago. They weren't the friendly type. Hassled my wife some when she was out fishing. They skeddadled when I started my motor and headed toward them."

"Sounds like them. Which way did they go? I'll give 'em hell when I catch up with 'em, okay?"

"Yeah, do that," the man said, pointing north.

Spence stared into the fire. *He would give them hell all right, the worst kind of living hell.*

*   *   *   *

The two men dropped Joe off at a motel bordering on Highway 17 in the middle of Kenora. "It's the only one in town where the bedbugs aren't big enough to eat you alive," one of the men had joked.

Joe appreciated the ride and the conversation. They were friendly and didn't pump him with a lot of questions.

It was 4:45 p.m. when Joe signed in. He planned to shower, shave, eat a light supper, and then hit one of the local taverns. He would start hitching to Winnipeg at 6:30 in the morning unless maybe his luck held, and he would meet someone who'd steer him onto a ride. He just hoped he could make it to Winnipeg in time to settle in and still get to the packing plant to apply for a job before the day's end.

*   *   *   *

The buzzing of chain saws tapered off throughout the forest. It was time to pick up the tools and end another long day of work. Rafe and Jake plodded toward their truck unaware that Louie had been trying to catch up with them.

"Hold up, you two," Louie shouted breathlessly. "Needa talk to ya. Why don't you come to my place for a few beers and supper?"

"Okay by me," Rafe said. "How about you, Jake?"

"Yeah. Got nothing better to do. And besides it's my week to cook."

"Good," Louie said. "Meet you at my house in a half hour. I've got a couple of things to do at the office. Then I'll be on my way. My wife'll keep you in cold ones till I get there."

As their truck bounced along the road to the cabin, Rafe and Jake wondered what ol' Louie wanted to talk to them about.

"Maybe he knows where Joe is," Jake suggested.

"Could be," Rafe said. "Maybe he's gonna give us a promotion—*or fire us?*"

"Guess we'll find out soon enough," Jake said, as he pulled the truck to the side of the cabin and stopped.

Louie's wife stood on the porch, ready to greet them. Rafe couldn't get used to calling her "Aunt." She didn't seem surprised that she had visitors. She must have known they were coming.

"Rough day, men?" she asked.

"Oh, about usual," Rafe answered. "Did Louie tell ya he wanted to see us?"

"Yeah, he did. Would ya like a beer?"

"You bet we would," Rafe said, tugging at his beard.

"Rafe, will you push me on my swing?" Louie's daughter screamed with glee from inside the kitchen.

"Sure, honey, soon as I get a beer."

She ran out of the cabin, letting the screen door slam. Racing to her tree swing, she squealed in anticipation of the high pushes Rafe had delighted in giving her at least once a week.

Later, after supper when his wife and daughter had gone for a canoe ride across the lake, Louie handed each of the men another beer.

"I'll say one thing," Rafe said. "Your wife's a helluva lot better cook than Jake is."

"Don't expect an argument from me," Jake laughed. "It was mighty good chow."

"Guess I'm spoiled," Louie said, plopping down on the couch, facing the other two in easy chairs.

"So what do you want to talk about?" Rafe asked.

"Well," Louie seemed in no hurry to get on with the conversation, "I've been thinking about Joe running out on yas. And I'm wondering why you guys seem to care so much? All the questions around camp and all?"

"So what's the problem? He *is* my brother, you know."

"Can't quite put my finger on it, but maybe it has something to do with this." He got up from the couch and walked over to a bookshelf where a pile of old newspapers rested on top. Pulling one out from the bottom of the stack, he faced the two of them and read: "Murderers Commit Mayhem in Boundary Waters."

Rafe and Jake glanced nervously toward one another. Rafe felt a burning sensation in his stomach and lower esophagus, as he stared into Louie's eyes. "So why are you reading that to us? We heard some of the guys jawing about it when we first came here."

"You landed at my place shortly after that happened. Said you came through the Boundary waters. Just thought maybe you knew something about it," Louie said, searching his nephew's eyes.

"Do you think *we* did it? Is that it?" Rafe fumed.

"Naw! Naw! Just supposing."

"Well, quit supposing. Think we'd come here if we'da done something like that. Anyone who'da done that would be long gone from this area."

"Spose you're right," Louie mumbled, as he tossed the newspaper back on the top of the shelf.

"There you are supposin' again," Rafe said. "Of course, I'm right! We wouldn't be lookin' up any kin with the law on our tail, would we, Jake?"

"Hell, no," Jake said, trying to sound convincing. "I'd either head for the mountains or a big city like L.A. and lose myself in the crowd— nothing in between."

"And besides," Rafe retorted, "*what if we were the ones*. What would you do about it?"

"Now you're the one that's supposin'," Louie laughed, trying to hide his concern and wishing he had never confronted them so directly with the murder story. He had been wondering about their unexpected arrival for some time. He had never doubted that they had been running from some kind of trouble in the States. But he had figured it was something minor—never believing something as serious as murder, or at least not allowing himself to think it was murder. He hired all kinds of drifters who stayed working for a time and then disappeared. He never asked questions. It was better that way. And it provided him with cheap labor. So far, he had gained more than he lost by hiring men who lived on the seamy side of the law. As long as they did their work while they were there, it made for a profitable arrangement.

Relatives were different though. His curiosity had gotten the best of him. His sister had always considered him a loser because of his care-free lifestyle that had included three wives and a stint in prison for assault. But he had loved her, and where blood was concerned he was sensitive. He had known for years about Rafe's prison record, and he had been secretly *happy* to hear about it—partly because his brother-in-law had treated him like dirt more often than not—and partly because Rafe reminded him of his own life on the wild side. "You're telling me," he said, "that you had nothing to do with it, and that's good enough for me. Forget I even mentioned it." But he knew that he would not forget because when he had read the headlines to them, they had exchanged nervous glances. What he would do about it, he didn't know except pretend for the time being that he believed their story—for blood's sake—and the strong possibility that the *blood* might be his own.

"Sure thing," Rafe said. "Let's drink to it." The three of them clinked their beers together. Rafe eyed Louie intently, vowing to him-self to watch him more carefully, looking for any signs of betrayal. He wondered if he could safely trust anybody—with Joe running off, Jake getting more temperamental every day, and now this accusation by Louie.

"Oh, and by the way," Louie said, his voice faltering. "Some of my friends up Kenora way tell me a Yank fitting Joe's description passed through there day before yesterday. Likely he was heading to Win-nipeg, hoping to get a job at the meat packing plant there." Louie didn't tell them that he had been tracing Joe on his own, thinking Joe would be able to tell him something useful. And he was glad now that he had that little golden nugget to offer them. It would get their minds off his suspicion and back on Joe.

"You don't say," Rafe said, gulping down the last of his beer. Wiping the back of his hand across his beard, he looked at Jake. "My little brother's gonna play with some meat besides his own for a change. Ain't that something?"

"Sure is." Jake's dark eyes blinked rapidly. "He's likely to get all bloodied up on a job like that."

Louie knew they'd be after Joe; in fact, he had counted on it.

*   *   *   *

Spence celebrated his arrival in Canada by setting up camp earlier than usual. He would relax, get a good night's sleep and start out again in the morning. He felt reasonably sure that he had crossed the border in approximately the same area that his enemies had entered, avoiding customs' officials.

He wracked his brains in an attempt to remember any details in conversation from that nightmare on the island in Lake Alice. Any clues or hints that would pinpoint the murderers' destination. Something besides their *uncle's place*. At least he knew they were heading to a relative for sanctuary. But he didn't know their last names, and that would make his search more difficult. The unique description of the big redhead narrowed the odds down a little. And that's what he was counting on to spark peoples' memory. Anyone seeing that huge man with fire-red hair would remember him.

Spence would never forget his face. That much was certain. He would remember it even after he smashed it to a bloody pulp. That massive, freckled mug would blend in with his Vietnam nightmares for years to come. But he would have the satisfaction of knowing that it belonged to nothing alive.

*   *   *   *

Joe, his left hand covered with a steel-mesh glove, raked in the wobbly chunk of fat passing before him on the conveyor belt. After skimming off the little slivers of meat with his razor sharp knife, he flung the slimy layer of waste into one vat behind him and the scraps he had salvaged into another. Only his second night on the job and he hated it.

His particular task on the line had only taken him twenty-five minutes to learn and about two hours to master. It was the lowest paying job on the swing shift, but it paid him almost two dollars per hour more than he had been making working as a lumberjack. And it was all his. He didn't have to share it with anybody. He had been lucky enough to reach the plant in time to fill one of the last job openings.

"Can you start tonight?" the short, stocky man, smoking a cigar, had asked.

"I'll start right now, if you want," Joe had said.

"No. Your shift starts at 5:00. Be here at 4:30 to get your knife sharpened and find out what you're gonna be doing."

Joe's first night had gone fast mainly because of his anticipation of what the work would be like. But already during his second night he was bored. This was another job he would strike from his list of possible careers. Any job you can learn in twenty-five minutes can't be worth having for life.

The smell of bloody meat nauseated him, and the time he spent, whittling blobs of fat, passed by so slowly. The first night, a man observed his progress most of the four hour shift. He had given him a few pointers on how to keep his knife sharp, but that was about all the conversation that had been exchanged between them. Not much could go wrong on this job. And that was okay. He would just put in his time and save enough money to get back to the States. Maybe a month at tops. He would get away before Rafe caught up with him.

The room he had rented at a boarding house was not first class, but it came cheap, and because it was only five blocks away from the plant, he would not need transportation. He wondered what Rafe would think if he could see him now. Undoubtedly, he would be extremely angry. And that thought tickled Joe.

Now that his boss didn't check on him anymore, a tall, sinewy man working next to him pumped him with questions. He seemed to relish the fact that Joe was a Yank. And the more information that Joe told him, the more he meddled. His smart-ass ways reminded Joe of Jake's constant jibing.

"Look here, guys. We got us a Yank on the line," he shouted, causing those nearby to look his way. "A real-live-Yank."

Joe sensed the guy was baiting him, so he didn't volunteer anything. But it didn't matter. The man continued to rant.

"Bet you get a lot of pussy down there, or didn't your mommy tell you about that? I understand that girls lay down on the sidewalk and beg for it—from strangers even. Up here you won't get much 'cuz girls are uptight over Aids. Speakin' of that, you look like the kind of guy that only makes it with other guys." On and on he rattled, trying to fluster Joe.

At break time, Joe managed to avoid the man, but back on the line he continued his barrage of filthy insults. The man across from Joe didn't laugh, but he didn't say anything reassuring either. He stabbed his meat with his knife instead of pulling it in with his gloved hand—all the while keeping a formidable expression on his face. A naked lady was tattooed on his left arm and a serpent on his right. The lady danced when he flexed his muscles.

Joe felt alienated. He knew that if he were going to make it on that job he would have to do something about the *motor mouth* next to him. At first he thought ignoring the insults would quiet him down. But that didn't work. The man continued to berate him after their break, picking up where he had left off. The tattooed man across from him didn't seem the least bit amused by the filthy remarks that Joe endured, but he didn't say anything one way or the other. Joe didn't know what he thought.

Some of the other guys on both sides of the line laughed enough to encourage the jokester. Joe would have to shut him up or find another job. He couldn't take a month of that kind of shit. Fuming inside, he waited for the last hour of the swing shift when the rolls of fat got bigger and juicier. He hauled in a particularly large layer and sliced off the slivers of meat hiding in its folds.

"These sows are as slimy as the ones you fuck, huh, Yank?" the man to his left wisecracked.

Pretending indifference, Joe carved off the chunks of meat. After putting his knife in the hot water holder, he grabbed the bulky, juicy flab with both hands. He whipped the blubber hard, wrapping it around the man's face, completely covering his head. The man struggled, clawing the layer of pork from his face. He threw it back at Joe, but it slipped from his hands missing its mark.

"You fucker," he cried, lunging at Joe, his knife slashing the air. "I'm gonna carve off your balls for that."

Joe held his own. "And I'm gonna slice you into scrap meat and send you down to the waste barrel to be ground up for chicken feed. I've taken enough of your shit, *asshole*."

The man with the tattoos on his arms ran around to their side of the conveyor. Joe expected the worst. Two against one. But he was determined to end the nonsense, one way or the other.

The burly man approached them, fire in his eyes. Grabbing the big-mouth by the throat, he threatened him. "I'm tired of your filthy fucking mouth too. If the new guy don't kill ya, then I will."

Joe stood almost amused at the sight of his former tormentor, trembling in the grasp of two powerful arms. He had made an unexpected ally.

CHAPTER 20

▼

Spence walked along the gravel road, confident that it would lead him to a small town or at least a cabin where he could get some information. No cars or trucks had passed since he had stepped out of the woods onto the road an hour before. Removing his slouch hat, he wiped sweat from his forehead with the back of his hand. He stopped momentarily to readjust the straps of his backpack that dug into his shoulders. The position of the sun in the cloudless sky told him that it was close to eleven o'clock. He hoped he would engage people within the hour. But if he didn't, that was okay. He merely wanted to get his bearings and then work out a plan to search for his enemies. He had sunk his canoe in a small stream that fed into a mushroom-shaped lake. After weighting down the canoe with boulders, he felt assured that it would still be there when he needed it again. He had dug a hole nearby to hide his camping equipment, careful to camouflage his diggings, even though he didn't anticipate anyone stumbling on to his cache in such a remote area.

He had brought enough money to stay in motels for weeks if need be, and, if his funds ran out, he would send for more. Even if his quest consumed all of his savings, he would continue till it was over. *Till he faced those murderers one more time.* His nights had been filled with macabre dreams of the torture sessions at Lake Alice, laced with a hor-

rid amalgam of Vietnam nightmares. Often he had awakened screaming in his tent, pounding his bedroll with his fists, thinking he was
locked in a death struggle with one of his killers.

When his nights were not restful, that only made him more intent
by day. And that's the way he wanted it, forcing his mind to concentrate on his main objective—*to find and kill those butchers.*

Rounding a bend in the road, Spence saw what appeared to be a
general store, complete with a gas pump. A Ford pickup pulled out of
the driveway and lost itself in a dust cloud. Spence entered the building, hoping he could get the information he needed.

"Hi, stranger," a whiskered old man said, his arms resting on the
counter before him.

"Hi ya," Spence said, as he approached the area where four other
men sat on empty nail kegs playing cards on an old cable spool.

"What can I do for you?" the man asked.

"Well, first of all, I'd like something cold. Beer if you got any on
hand."

"Sure thing. Right in that cooler over there." The man pointed to a
faded blue cooler just beyond the card players.

Spence had not seen for years a contraption like this one holding
pop and beer. Rows of metal slats filled the interior along which bottles
hung by their caps, their contents soaking in cold water. After deposit-
ing four quarters, Spence guided a beer to the metal jaws that released
the bottle with a metallic snap. He opened it and took a few hearty
swigs. "Ah, that tastes good."

"Been traveling long?" the attendant asked.

"Yep. Quite a distance in that scorching sun." Spence eased his pack
on to the floor.

"Whatcha doing up this way, Yank?" one of the card players asked,
their card game interrupted.

"Just traveling. Seeing the sights. Doing a little fishing now and
then. I'm hoping to catch up with three guys from the States I met
crossing the Boundary Waters."

"Friends of yours?" the man behind the counter asked.

"I don't know them that well, but they said they'd be heading this way and maybe we'd get together and have a few beers." Spence was careful not to call them *friends*, knowing from his past experiences that anyone meeting those thugs was generally happy to be rid of them.

"Three of 'em, huh?" The old man scratched his whiskers in reflection. "What do they look like?"

"One of them is a big red headed guy. Another has long black hair, and the third is a few years younger—maybe twenty-one or two. Nice looking kid. Mighta passed through here about seven weeks ago." Spence looked toward the card players as he gave them the descriptions.

"Nope. Nobody like that been through here or we'd have remembered them. Right boys?" The card player who had spoken before looked to the rest of the men who nodded in agreement.

"Well, thanks anyway," Spence said, taking a swig from his beer. "But, say, these guys sure talked a lot about women. Where would a guy go around here to have a good time?"

"Most everyone around here parties at the Pine Ridge Lodge about fifteen miles to the north. This road here will get you close. You can get further directions in a little town ten miles away." The old man gestured toward the place somewhere down the road.

"Thanks again." Spence put his empty beer bottle in the rack. "Guess I'll be on my way."

"That's a long hike, Yank. Fergy here can give you a lift most of the way," the old man offered.

"Sure thing," a burly man said, focusing his eyes on his cards. "My wife doesn't like me coming late to lunch. I'll be going as soon as we finish this hand."

*   *   *   *

Spence signed into the lodge, deciding to stay the night. He wanted to check out the action in the bar during the evening scene. He found his rustic room comfortable. Not much furniture, save a desk, luggage rack, and king-size bed. After a refreshing cold shower, he headed toward the restaurant. A beef dinner would be good, especially if it tasted home-cooked as advertised. He wallowed in the free time he had on his hands. Scanning the room, he noticed most of the diners were elderly. He hoped the bar would attract the kind of young, healthy guys he was stalking *for the sole purpose of killing them.* His waitress was a young, dimple-cheeked brunette who smiled constantly, spreading cheer to each table she served.

"When does this place get lively, Miss, or am I witnessing the action now?" Spence helped her clear the dishes away from his table.

"The restaurant never really gets on fire," she said, a twinkle in her eyes, "but the bar starts picking up at 5:00, and by 9:00 people are standing in line to dance."

"Well, I guess I'll just have to wait around for the excitement."

She smiled broadly and hurried off toward the kitchen with a tray of dishes.

Spence ambled over to the saloon area and took a peek. It was larger than he had imagined it to be. He could see the possibilities the place offered. A horseshoe-shaped bar with a spacious dance floor. Very accommodating. He could almost see the faces of his adversaries sitting at the bar sneering at him.

Spence wiled away the afternoon reading newspapers and dosing in the shade, as he stretched out in a chair by the outdoor swimming pool. At 4:30, he sauntered into the bar and sat on a stool opposite the doorway. He wanted to check out all incoming patrons without being too obvious. What would he do if saw the big redhead and the others? Would he confront them in the saloon? Probably not, unless they recognized him. He wondered if they knew that he had survived the ordeal at Lake Alice. He hoped that he was *dead* as far as they were concerned. His chances of tracking them to their quarters would be greater that way. He would like to deal with them in private.

Sipping his scoop of beer, Spence watched as the bar filled up just like the waitress had predicted. He had asked the bartender earlier if he had remembered seeing the three men he sought. The man checked with his helpers. None of them seemed to have any recollection of the men in question. Spence bided his time drinking beer and nibbling on cheese and crackers. Had he drawn a blank? Maybe he should turn in for the night and get an early start in the morning.

One of the bartenders approached him and asked if wanted any more beer.

"Yeah, one more," Spence said, shoving a dollar toward him.

The man plunked down the beer and leaned toward Spence to talk above the din. "Did you say one of those guys was a big redhead?"

"Yeah, and one has long black hair. His eyes twitch nervously now and then. The other one is a good looking kid about twenty-one or so."

"Well, I only recall the redhead. He got into a little trouble here about two weeks ago. He was pinching girls on their behinds till a boyfriend called him on it. We had to throw him out. Haven't seen him since."

"Do you know where they live?"

"Nope. Never saw them before that night. You might talk to Jurgen—our German bouncer, standing over by the door. He helped to see them on their way."

"Thanks," Spence said.

"Are they friends of yours?" the bartender asked.

"No. Let's just say they owe me." Spence gulped down his beer and added a dollar to his change for a tip.

He picked his way through the crowd, easing up to the huge man leaning against the wall, his arms folded in front of him.

"Pierre tells me that you might be able to help me out," Spence said, his voice all but drowned out by the music from the stereo on the dance floor.

"How's that?" the big man said, cuffing his ear.

"You bounced a big red-headed guy out of here two weeks ago. Remember?" Spence shouted.

"Ya. He was a bad man. Caused trouble with the ladies. Why do you want him?"

"He owes me some money, and I want to collect. Do you know where he lives?"

"No. I have not seen him again. The three of them drove away in a truck. It had an insignia for a logging camp on its side. A French name, I think. I still get them mixed up. I have been in Canada only one year."

"*Paydirt,*" Spence thought, as he thanked the man for the information and headed toward his room. A lumber camp. There couldn't be just too many around. And even if there were hundreds, He would check them all out. At least he had *something* to go on.

After reaching his room, he plopped on the bed and thumbed through the yellow pages in the phone book. Looking under *Lumber*, Spence counted four names. None appeared to be French. But under *Logging*, he spotted two names that were definitely French—Broussard's Logging Camp and Renoux's Saw Mill. In the morning, he would start with Broussard. Maybe he would get lucky.

After checking out of the motel, Spence headed toward a bait shop where he hoped to get more information about the surrounding territory. The clerk at the desk had suggested that he go there since his own knowledge of the forest was limited.

"You'll find some guys there who hunt and fish in these parts," the man had said, happy that he could help in some way.

Spence approached the store after a twenty-minute walk. The place seemed lively for 6:00 a.m. There were two cars parked at the gas pumps out in front, and people were coming and going from other vehicles in the driveway. Inside the store, customers mingled among the rows of shelves stocked with groceries, fishing, and hunting equipment.

Since he wasn't sure how long he would be camping outdoors, Spence decided to buy a few canned goods to supplement the fish that he knew he would catch. He also remembered that he should get a Canadian fishing license. He didn't want any hassles with the law—not when he might be within striking distance of his prey.

After picking up what food he might need, he stood in line at the checkout counter. A stocky mustached man in a white T-shirt and jeans stood at the register punching keys, a sour look on his face. He didn't offer friendly talk with his customers unless he knew them personally. When Spence asked for a fishing license, the man acted like he was doing him a favor by getting it out of a drawer in the counter.

"Year round or seasonal?" he said, looking annoyed that someone had broken his steady ringing of sales at the register.

"Year round," Spence said. "And have you got a local map or guide?"

"Cost you a dollar extra," the man snarled.

"I'll take it." Spence looked the man square in the eyes.

Stepping outside into the morning sunlight, Spence walked over to a picnic table under a large pine tree. Either that guy was nursing a hell-of-a hangover, or he was a rotten businessman—maybe both, but he didn't want to waste any more time thinking about him.

After stashing his new supplies in his backpack, he spread the map out on the table. It was not as detailed as he would have liked, but at least it would allow him to get his bearings. It did include Broussard's Logging Camp and the woods and lake surrounding it—and that was his main objective for the time being.

While hitchhiking along the gravel road to the west, Spence toyed with thoughts of being picked up by his enemies. He could see himself bouncing along in the back end of their truck with them in the cab unaware that he was the man they had supposedly killed. His slouch

Then again, he wondered if those murderers ever thought anymore about what they had done. Would they even remember him at all? Were they the type who plowed through life one day at a time—creating havoc wherever they went and never looking back. No guilt, no compassion. Just forging ahead leaving a trail of blood and destruction until someone stopped them. He had met his share of people like that in Nam. He would stop them all right. He would put them out of business permanently, but they would have time to regret their past actions. He would make them beg for mercy. He would make them do whatever he wanted them to do. But they couldn't satisfy the one thing that really mattered. *They couldn't bring Marna or any of the others back to life*. And that would be the only way for them to atone for their evil actions on this side of the grave. But he knew he could not rest until he ripped the life from their bodies. He didn't know how he would feel once he had wreaked the vengeance he so eagerly desired. *He did know that he couldn't live without it.*

A truck barreled down the road, kicking up gravel and leaving a trail of dust. The driver stared at Spence but didn't slow down—if anything, he speeded up as he was passing him. The cautious type, Spence thought. And that was okay as far as he was concerned. It paid to be careful on the road these days—both for drivers and hitchhikers. Every day, unwary travelers find a stopping place in the morgue. It was happening all too frequently. Weirdoes of all kinds *get off* on harassing unsuspecting people.

Spence waited for the truck to get swallowed up in the distance. He continued when the air cleared once again, stopping momentarily to adjust the straps that made his shoulders ache.

Another pickup truck roared past him, but the driver slammed on his brakes, skidding ten feet on the gravel. He backed up to where Spence stood. A passenger in the truck looked Spence over carefully. "Where are ya headed, mister?"

"Lake Blue," Spence said. "Am I going in the right direction?" He knew that he was, and he didn't want to mention the logging camp outright.

"Yeah, it's ten or fifteen miles down the road. We'll be going right by it. Want a lift?"

"Sure, I won't have to eat so much dust that way."

"Throw your gear in the back and hop in the cab."

Spence did as he was told. It was crowded in the seat, but it beat walking.

"Gonna do a little fishing, huh?" the driver said, as he gunned down the road.

"Yeah, just take it easy for a few days. Hope I catch some."

"Don't worry. The fish are hungry at Lake Blue. It's not fished out like some of the resort lakes."

"You're a Yank, aren't ya?" the man next to him asked.

"Yep. Thought I'd get a little change of scenery," Spence said, anticipating the next question.

"Lake Blue is way out in the middle of nowhere, if it's privacy you're looking for," the driver said. "No one'll be bothering you out there. Lest you go to the far west end. There's a logging camp that gets close on that side. A lot of coming and going with trucks and dozers."

"Thanks for the tip," Spence said, knowing that's exactly where he would be heading. He talked as little as possible, merely answering all their questions politely. They seemed to buy his fishing story and didn't probe any further about why a man alone would travel to virtually unknown Lake Blue.

When they got as close as they could to the lake, the driver stopped the truck and pointed into the woods. "Two miles that way will get you to Lake Blue. Enjoy yourself. You'll catch enough fish all right."

"Thanks," Spence said, removing his pack from the truck. He waited till the truck sped around a bend then he forged into the timber heading for the lake. Now that he was close to the camp, he didn't want to be seen by passersby. He knew he had taken a chance hitching a ride like that, but he wanted to reach the lumber camp before the workers, so he could check them out before they spread into the forest. Walking directly north, he soon spotted the waters of Lake Blue off in the distance. He remained behind the cover of trees and followed the lake's shoreline to its western extremity where he knew Broussard's Lumber Camp was located.

*   *   *   *

Spence lay on his stomach on a cliff overlooking the forest below. Partially concealed by scraggy shrubs, he scanned the logging operation with his binoculars. The sun was behind him, so there would be no reflection off the glasses.

He had settled in on the ledge, waiting for the workers to arrive, hoping to get a glimpse of his enemies before they scattered into the forest. Three trucks pulled into a small clearing. The men slowly got their tools ready for the day's work. They joked about Friday night escapades, their voices carrying up to Spence who froze in his spot.

After scrutinizing each man, and not seeing his enemies, he wondered if they worked at this particular camp. Then again, he reasoned that it was Saturday and maybe the full crew didn't have to show up. What would he do if they didn't appear on the scene? He couldn't very well ask any of the others if the men he sought worked there. Not when he intended to kill them. But how long should he wait? He decided he would stay for one more hour. If they didn't arrive by then, he would find a secluded spot to set up camp and check out the crew again on Monday.

The workers spread out and disappeared into the verdant forest. Soon after, the agonizing whine of chain saws interrupted the stillness of the morning air. Limbs from giant pine trees snapped as they crashed through branches from other trees before hitting the ground. Each new sound of the morning's activities registered with Spence, patiently viewing the valley below him.

Out of the corner of his eye, he sighted a blue pickup grinding its way along the dirt road toward the clearing where the other trucks were parked. A ray of hope spread across his face as he eyed the moving vehicle. When it finally came to a halt, he tensed, as he watched the door on the driver's side swing open. He refocused his binoculars and zeroed in on the tall redhead who stretched his arms above his head and looked up toward the cliff, *unaware that he was being watched by his executioner.* Spence recognized the other man as one of his captors too. Both their names came to him. *Rafe* and *Jake.* So now they were his. He thought how easy it would be for him to pick them off with his rifle. But he had packed only his .45, and besides, shooting them was too easy of a way for those two to die. They must die slowly and painfully, all the while knowing who it was that was executing them. Spence knew that Lady Luck had smiled upon him. He had anticipated a much longer search for the murderers. He had envisioned many months in pursuit—maybe even years. But he had prepared himself mentally for the duration of his quest—no matter how long it might take. Now *they* were standing among the trees beneath him. Adrenaline flowed through his body. He chuckled sardonically.

But the good feelings were soon overcome by the chilling hate that pulsed through his brain. He had to force himself to stay put—to keep from rising up and screaming, "I'm coming for you bastards." Trying to control his emotions, his body stiffened and he sensed that he was about to black out. "No! No!" he groaned. "Not this time. I'm gonna take it out on your skulls." His chin scraped on the rocky ground as he rolled over onto his back. Clenching his fists and looking straight at the cloudless sky seemed to momentarily clear his head.

CHAPTER 21

▼

Spence stretched out on the cliff watching the burly redhead sawing through logs, unaware that he was being observed through powerful binoculars. Occasionally Spence would lose sight of his prey, as he ventured behind a thick screen of trees. Two hours had already passed, but Spence was not the least bit impatient. He felt excited knowing that he had tracked down his enemies so soon. They were within striking distance. He had only to wait for the right moment. He didn't want to botch their execution. Everything must go according to his plans.

As he lay there on the rocky surface, Spence remembered an experience from Vietnam whereby he had observed an enemy camp for eight hours, waiting for the precise moment to attack with maximum surprise. He had been patient then too, getting irritated only when some of his men got restless and careless. They wanted to attack immediately to avoid prolonging their agony, as they lay on the jungle floor, mosquitoes and leeches feasting on their bodies. Spence convinced them they should wait for the appropriate moment when the enemy had bedded down for the night. He had hoped that his troops would sustain only minimal casualties if they caught the enemy by surprise after nightfall. And he had been right; his platoon scored thirty-two kills that night while he lost only one man.

Rage slowly filled his body as he watched Rafe lumbering through the trees. He wanted so much to sneak up on him and kill him—slit his throat, letting his warm blood ooze through his fingers to the ground, as he had done to so many enemy soldiers in Vietnam. But that would be too quick. Rafe must know who was to be his executioner—and have plenty of time to squirm in the face of death. He must taste the same kind of fear that the girls had felt before they were butchered.

Shortly before noon, the men headed toward their trucks—tools in hand. Did that mean they were knocking off for the day or moving to a new location? Spence had to hurry. He wanted to get down to the first fork in the road and wait for Rafe and Jake to pass him there. He would follow them as quickly as he could, hoping they wouldn't outdistance him too much. Maybe he could find a vantage point on a high knoll so he could pinpoint where they lived. If not, he would have to keep searching down each turn-off until he spotted their truck parked at a cabin or camp of some kind. According to his map of the area, only one main road penetrated the forest, so any branch off would be a relatively short lane to a dwelling.

Spence hurried down from the overhanging cliff and cut a straight diagonal path to the road. He moved as swiftly as his pack would allow till he reached the first fork in the road. There he waited for Rafe and Jake to pass by. From a small hilltop he watched stretches of the road for a few miles ahead.

As the Ford barreled along the dusty gravel road, Spence followed it every inch of the way with his binoculars. He had climbed into a tree at the top of the hill overlooking the road. He recognized Jake on the passenger side.

*   *   *   *

"Son-of-a-bitch! The morning dragged," Jake said, flicking the ashes from his cigarette out the window. "I must have sweat out ten gallons of beer."

"Can't say that my morning went fast either," Rafe said. "I had a funny feeling that someone was watching me. Kinda strange."

"Maybe it was a vulture thinking you were dead because you were dragging your ass so much," Jake laughed.

"Fuck you! I've got the same feeling right now. I can't explain it."

"Well, keep driving and get me home before something gobbles us up. I want to have one more beer 'fore I die," Jake snickered.

*   *   *   *

Joe Johnson slipped into the front seat of the car he had rented earlier in the day. *Rent-a-wreck-Cheap* the sign had flashed in front of the lot. The salesman had rambled on and on about the good condition of the car. Joe was not so sure the car would make the trip he had planned. The tappets were obviously loose, creating a considerable clicking sound.

Would the car make it even one way to Broussard's Lumber Camp? Or would it break down somewhere on the road. Joe guessed that it didn't make much difference. He didn't have much to lose. He had rented it for the weekend for $24.95—cheaper than a bus and more convenient than hitching. He had wanted to reach Rafe's cabin sometime after nightfall. He would tell his brother exactly why he left and why he was going to lone it in the future. He had decided that he owed him that much at least. He would even mention that he planned to go back to the States as soon as he had saved a little traveling money. He wouldn't have to say where he intended to roost because he wasn't sure of that himself—even though sunny California seemed to be beckoning to him.

He knew Rafe would be in his usual rage and maybe even get rough with him. But he also knew that he himself was more independent now. He was not going to back down under any circumstances, and he was not going to take any physical abuse either. He would keep his .45 handy just in case. He hoped he wouldn't need that, but he also remembered how difficult it was to reason with his hot-tempered brother. Rafe had intimidated him for years, as he had done to almost anyone who disagreed with him. Joe could trace Rafe's turning sour back to the time in high school when his first serious love affair had gone wrong. He had never been the same after losing his girl and his football scholarship to college. It was like his mind had snapped. A vice of anger and bitterness held him firmly in its grip. All the hopes and all the dreams he had of playing college football and maybe getting a shot with the pros drained out of him. Only once in a while when he was drunk did he ever refer to *what could have been.*

But Joe couldn't let those old tender feelings he had for Rafe stand in the way of what he intended to do. He would confront him for one last time—*mano a mano*—and then make his break, clean and simple. No sneaking away and hiding, wondering when Rafe would find him and try to force him back into a man on the run from the law. If his brother had any feelings left for him, then he would understand that he must be allowed to go free and start living a decent life before it was too late. Rafe owed him that much. And if he didn't want to part as friends, then so be it. But he was going his own way.

So immersed in thought as he sped down the blacktop highway snaking through the pine tree forest, Joe skidded the car around a bend and nearly lost control. Better slow down. He didn't want a ticket and the hassle that went with it. He had plenty of time to get where he was going.

*   *   *   *

Spence remained in the tree, his eyes pressed to the binoculars as he followed the blue pickup down the road. He had hoped they would swing to the right because he could see farther that way. He could still hear the roar of the truck as it gunned out of sight around a bend in the road. Quickly he scanned the area for the next visible stretch, and there he paused, waiting to catch sight of it again. But it never happened.

His ears picked up the slower pull of the engine and finally the noise tapering off entirely. They had stopped. Were they at their cabin? Spence kept his eyes on the open stretch of road just in case.

He heard two truck doors slam. He waited, but he had a feeling of satisfaction that they had arrived at their destination. After ten minutes when he could neither hear nor see them, he decided it was safe to climb down from his perch and get a closer look. Upon reaching the ground, he shouldered his pack and crept toward the clump of trees where the truck had disappeared. The distance was only a half-mile, but Spence took his time, stopping now and then to listen for sounds of a motor starting up. Hearing nothing except birds chirping, he continued till he observed a cabin in a clearing beyond the trees. After creeping slowly to the edge of the tree line, he lay flat in the tangle of weeds and bushes that lined the perimeter of the grassy opening. He could sense movement through the window of the cabin. If they spotted him, he'd have to take them right away in the daylight. He hoped that would not be the case. He wanted to capture them after nightfall when his chances of being interrupted would be less—much less.

He lay there in the weeds staring at the cabin for at least an hour. So this was their hideout. He knew he had been lucky to zero in on his enemies so soon. He wondered what their plans might be for the day. If he knew his quarry as well as he thought he did, they would not spend the day cooped up in that cabin. He was surprised that they had remained indoors for so long already. Maybe they were having lunch before they ventured into town or wherever they planned to spend their Saturday.

Spence froze when their cabin door opened, and Rafe and Jake appeared—each holding a can of beer. They climbed into their truck and headed down the lane toward the road where they turned in the direction of the next town. After waiting several minutes until he was sure they would not be returning, Spence stood up, brushed himself off, and walked toward the cabin. He looked in a window to make sure the third man was not at home. *Where was he anyway?* Did he work at another job, or had he split from the other two? Maybe they were going to meet him some place.

Spence tried the door latch, and finding it unlocked, he stepped inside the cabin. A musty odor combined with the aftermath of lunch smells stunk up the cabin. Slowly he moved about studying the layout. He was very careful not to disturb anything so they wouldn't realize they had had a visitor. He did handle the 12-gauge shotgun that he found leaning against the wall between two bunk beds, careful to put it back just the way he found it. He removed the shells, shoving them into his pocket. He chuckled softly to himself at the remains of pork and beans and fried hamburger left in the pans on the stove where several flies had gathered. He wondered if that was Rafe and Jake's steady diet. *It was as good as any food for a last meal, he supposed.*

Walking by a window, he glanced toward the road. He didn't want to be caught in the cabin. A mistake like that might cost him his life, as his carelessness had almost done to him at Lake Alice. His brain registered the entire outlay of the cabin interior—where every piece of furniture rested and where the fireplace sat in relationship to the beds and the kitchen area. The absence of a telephone would be to his advantage; he would not have to snip the wire before his planned assault—one less detail to worry about. He had already noticed where the single electrical wire entered the cabin; he could knock that out in a minute when the time was right. Confident that he had the necessary details of the cabin fixed in his mind, he slipped outside and explored the surrounding area. He wanted to get the feel of the yard so that he wouldn't stumble over some object in the dark. *And it would be dark come nightfall.* No moon to light the area, making him an easy target. On the backside of the cabin, he found a rabbit hutch containing several rabbits. They must be for eating purposes—these guys wouldn't have them for pets.

Satisfied, that he had scrutinized the lay of the land and the cabin itself, Spence drifted into the forest. He walked to the spot where he had hidden his pack. Slipping it over his shoulders, he trudged deeper into the woods. He would cook himself some fish, that is, if he could catch some, and then he would explore further the entire area, in case he would be forced to take an alternate route out of there after he— *after he what?* After he killed those butchers and left their bodies to rot on the cabin floor and their goddamned souls to rot in Hell!

He gritted his teeth as anger welled up inside him. He couldn't wait to render those murderers helpless and make them suffer the way they had made the girls and him suffer. He would avenge their humiliation, torture and death. It was payback time. He remembered how good he had felt in Vietnam when he had the opportunity to kill soldiers whom he knew were responsible for merciless torture and slaughter of innocents. He would feel even better tonight when he stood as judge and executioner over those evil men who had raped and murdered four innocent girls.

Wiping a tear from his cheek as he thought of lovely Marna, he vowed that they would beg for mercy before he was through with them. And he would hear their cries and wallow in their misery.

Intent upon the annihilation of his enemies, as he tromped through the underbrush, Spence noticed movement in some berry bushes ahead of him. He froze, wondering if he had come upon men or animals. Two young black bears romped into a clearing. Spence quickly scanned the area for the mother he sensed would be nearby. He knew better than to be caught between her and her young ones. That would put him in danger that might force him to shoot the mother—and he didn't want to attract that kind of attention to himself with the gunshots. Spotting her off to his right, lumbering away from him, Spence carefully trekked in the opposite direction. The bear had not picked up his scent as yet, or she would have come running to protect her offspring. The young bears continued their play in total detachment, oblivious to his presence. That was in his favor, for if they showed fear, then Spence would have to shoot to kill because the mother would charge him immediately.

After walking slowly but steadily for about a mile, and feeling assured that he was out of danger, he knifed through the woods toward the lake.

*   *   *   *

"Hey, Jake, what d'ya say we shoot some pool at the Pitstop 'fore we chase us some pussy?" Rafe eased the pickup into a diagonal parking space.

"Might as well. Maybe we'll run into a couple of hot bitches here. I've seena few hanging around just asking for it. Not bad looking either."

They entered the saloon, and after adjusting their eyes to the darkness, they sat down on stools at the middle of the bar. They were content that the place was more crowded than usual for early Saturday afternoon. Some of the people belonged to a wedding party filling in time between the marriage and the reception. Two bridesmaids in their formal dresses were playing pool, laughing and drinking beer. Rafe and Jake gave one another a knowing look, as if to say that prospects for latching on to a woman looked pretty good.

"What are ya gonna do about your brother?" Jake asked.

"Thought I told ya yesterday. We're going on Monday to Winnipeg. Louie said it was okay, if we both went, as long as we're back on time for Tuesday."

"No. You didn't tell me, but it's okay with me. I can use a long weekend. This logging shit is starting to get to me."

"Can't say that I like it either, but at least we're safe for the time being. That is, if Joe hasn't spilled his guts to somebody who might want to be a hero and turn us in."

"I don't think he'd do that," Jake said, slurping beer from the foaming mug before him, "for two reasons. First, he was in on the party back on the island, and second, we'd waste the fucker—*and he knows it.*"

"Yeah, you're right. But just the same, I want to get my hands on him and teach him a lesson for running off."

"What are ya gonna do, Rafe? Just go into that meat packing plant and haul him away?"

"Naw, I'd like to, but that's not smart. We'll jump him when he gets off work and persuade my little brother, one way or another, to come back here with us."

"Count on me to help you shanghai him. I don't think he'll come peacefully."

"Spose not," Rafe said, conscious of a woman who staggered into him. He hooked her with his arm, and when she didn't resist, he lowered his hand to her rump and gave it a squeeze.

"Hi, cowboy," she slurred. "Want some company?"

*   *   *   *

Joe parked his noisy heap at a roadside cafe. No sense hurrying. He knew Rafe and Jake would not be home until late that night—not unless they could convince some women to spend the night with them in their smelly cabin. He would have a few beers, eat a steak sandwich, and then continue on his way to the cabin and wait for Rafe to arrive. He hoped that his brother wouldn't be too drunk. He knew only too well how hard he was to reason with after he had been on a drinking binge. Maybe he would be so out of it that he could convince him to go to sleep and talk things over in the morning. Or maybe he should stay overnight in a motel and confront Rafe in the morning? But then he remembered how ornery Rafe could be nursing a hangover. And besides, he wanted to get an early start back to Winnipeg. There probably wasn't a *good* time to tell Rafe what his plans were. Sometimes his brother mellowed out if he didn't drink too much. That's all he could hope for under the circumstances.

*   *   *   *

Spence had chanced a small fire because the night had turned cool and damp. His campsite was over a mile from the cabin and the flames would be concealed from the road by the surrounding timber. He sat there glaring at the burning logs, mesmerized by their glow. His mind drifted to the night that he had spent with the girls on Lake Alice. He remembered again how pleased they had been when he had built a huge fire on the beach. Their friendly banter and later his walk with Marna. It was then that he had sensed his growing attraction for her. A pleasure that he had not allowed himself for sometime with other women he had met.

A crackling log toppled from another one, creating a flurry of sparks. The diversion changed his mood from what was bordering on self-pity to one of hatred for the fiendish murderers he would be killing soon. In a few hours it would all be over with. Two vicious rats would be dead. The world would be two bastards short. It wouldn't bring back the victims of their savagery, but at least no one else would suffer at their hands. And after he had the pleasure of killing those vermin, *then what?* Where would he go? What would he do? Go back to teaching? No, not for a while anyway. Maybe some day in another location. He didn't rule it out entirely. He would travel across Canada and spend some time in the Rockies. He had never been there before. Would the law come after him? Would he feel hunted all his life—a man on the run? Or would he be able to settle down and put these past few months out of his mind? He hadn't been able to forget Vietnam after more than ten years, so why would this be any different? But just maybe it wouldn't be the same. Maybe he could get caught up in living again. He would just have to wait and see after this night was over.

*   *   *   *

Spence sat on the damp ground resting his back against a tree. Occasionally, he rubbed his upper body vigorously to ward off the night chill. He had left the comfort of his campfire an hour before and checked to see if the pickup was parked next to the cabin. He assumed that he would have heard it rumbling up the gravel road in the stillness of the night, but he wanted to make sure. There would be no slip-ups this time. Satisfied they had not arrived home, he waited patiently about ten yards from the clearing. He made sure that the headlights from the truck would not reveal him.

Spence had gone over his plan time after time. All he needed now were the other participants. But they would be coming, and he hoped they would be alone; otherwise, he would have to wait for another night.

The whine of a truck engine off in the distance alerted him. The sounds got closer and closer, and soon headlights flashed on the front of the cabin. It was *them*.

Both men got out of the truck and relieved themselves on the grass.

"Jesus, it's getting fuckin' cold," Jake said.

"Yeah. Too bad things didn't work out better with those bitches back in town," Rafe said, zipping up his jeans. "Cockteasers. Both of 'em. They don't know how fuckin' lucky they were that we didn't jump 'em when they left that tavern."

"Well, I sure scared the shit out of that one. I squeezed one of her tits so hard she started crying."

"I heard her. Thought she was gonna call the bartender, but she just stomped out to her car. Probably just as well. We don't need any more trouble our way."

After entering the cabin, they turned on a light and started a fire. Spence, having moved to the edge of the clearing, stretched out on the ground and waited. It bothered him that the young guy was not with them? Would he be coming later? He would have to be wary of his possible return.

Every once in a while he could hear muffled laughter spilling through the closed cabin windows. It would take a while for those guys to settle in for the night. But that was okay. They were right where he wanted them to be.

An hour later, someone turned out the light in the cabin. The glow from the fireplace shone through the window. Spence licked his lips in anticipation. The games were about to begin. Still, he waited for another half-hour.

Opening his backpack, he reached in and grabbed a handful of gravel he had deposited earlier in the day. He tossed a few pieces underhand to the top of the cabin roof, listening to them as they rattled down the other side over where he knew Rafe and Jake would be sleeping.

"What was that?" Rafe bellowed.

"How the fuck do I know?" Jake grumbled. "Maybe a squirrel working the night shift."

Spence waited several minutes and then threw another handful of rocks onto the top of the roof. He then stepped back into the trees and watched as Rafe ran out the front door of the cabin in his underwear, a flashlight in his hand. He jumped clear of the porch and shined the light at the rooftop. Finally, he snorted and went back inside.

"What was it?" Jake asked.

"I dunno. Didn't see a fuckin' thing."

Spence paused at the base of the utility pole and glanced toward the cabin window. After the cabin darkened once again, he shinned up the pole and cut the wire so that it would fall toward the road side and not in the cabin clearing. Then he crept stealthily to the corner of the cabin where he knew he could climb up to the roof. He listened for sounds coming from the interior, and realizing the quietude, he made his ascent. He clomped noisily along the cabin's peak, stopping now and then for effect, and then ran and dived into an overhanging pine tree.

"Jesus Chr-r-rist! There's someone on top of the roof," Rafe screamed, pulling a .45 from its holster under his bed. Before Jake could stop him, he fired twice up through the ceiling. "That oughtta scare the mother fucker."

"Jesus!" Jake shrieked, pulling on his jeans. He grabbed for the shotgun and ran outside. Rafe was right behind him with the .45 in one hand and the flashlight in the other. They scrambled in opposite directions around the cabin and met on the far side.

"See anything?" Rafe's breath came in short pants.

"Nope! I didn't." Jake eyed the woods at the back of the cabin.

"Well, somebody's playing games with us, and if they want to see the sun come up, they'd better get the fuck outta here." Rafe screamed loud enough for their unseen adversary to hear. Then they both marched back to the front of the cabin.

"What's the matter with the goddamn light?" Rafe flicked the switch up and down several times.

"Musta cut the line."

"We're gonna get whoever's playin' games, if we have to stay up all night," Rafe growled.

Spence waited a half-hour before he started calling from the protection of the forest. "Ra-a-a-f-f-f-f-e. I've come to get yo-o-o-u-u-u-!"

"Why, that cocksucker! Give me the shotgun." Rafe grabbed the weapon from Jake, and pushing open the door, he stepped onto the porch and, after pointing the gun toward the woods where he thought the sound had come from, he pulled both triggers. The hammers clicked twice.

"Christ! Who unloaded my gun?" Feeling his way back into the cabin, he returned with a handful of shells. He stuffed two into the open chambers of his gun and blasted both barrels into the surrounding trees. Removing the spent cartridges, he reloaded and fired away again. He repeated the process till he was out of ammunition.

"Do you want to kill them?"

"What do you mean *them*?"

"It's probably just some of the guys from work, half pissed up."

"They're gonna have a few leaks in 'em, if they keep fucking around." Rafe's voice rang through the forest, as he stumbled back into the dark of the cabin, heading for more shells.

Spence heard the buckshot spraying the trees in front of him just out of range. His enemies were panicking. That was good. He circled way around to the side of the cabin and lurked in the bushes. He could see a light dodging around in the cabin. Slowly he crept up to the cabin, and, ducking under a window, he headed for the front porch. Silently he skipped the step that he knew squeaked and stood before the door. He rapped his knuckles on the door twice and then vanished into the darkness along side the cabin, holding his breath.

Rafe, shotgun in hand, ran outside and jumped off the porch. He made a wide turn around the corner, screaming, "Okay, fucker, I've got...."

His sentence was cut short by a swift kick in the groin, as strong hands yanked the gun from his grasp. The stock of the gun thudded against his jaw, knocking him to the ground.

Spence dropped the shotgun and pulled Rafe to his feet. Half dragging him, half carrying him, he shoved his limp body through the open door. Jake quickly flashed the light toward the commotion. Upon seeing Rafe, he held his fire. Spence pushed Rafe who was semi-conscious toward the light and sent him sprawling on top of Jake. Then grabbing Jake by the hair, he smashed his fist into his face and followed that with a blow to his throat, causing him to drop the .45.

Seizing the flashlight that had rolled practically under one of the beds, Spence checked the condition of his two victims. Rafe lay completely silent like a massive bear rug. Jake moaned and tried to get to his feet. Spence deftly kicked him on the side of his head rendering him unconscious.

Shining the light before him, Spence maneuvered to the kitchen. He struck a match, lighting the Coleman lantern, resting on the shelf above the stove. Tossing the flashlight on the table, he carried the lantern over to the two lifeless bodies. Seeing they would keep for a few minutes, he hurried outside to his backpack he had stashed around the corner just off the porch. He grabbed two coils of rope and ran back inside.

Trussing up his two captives, he bound their hands and feet, and then, one by one, he hoisted them to a standup position by throwing two ropes over one of the cabin beams. They hung there with their hands over their heads like two rag dolls. Now they were finally at his mercy. Spence had longed for this moment. Those suckers were as good as dead.

Spence stoked up the glowing coals in the fireplace and added more logs. Approaching the two limp bodies dangling from their ropes, he sliced off their clothes with his hunting knife and then sat by the fire, waiting to see their eyes open. Growing impatient with their slow arousal, he walked over to the pump at the sink and filled a plastic bucket with water. He eyed his two captives for a few seconds and then doused each in the face with cold water. Jake mumbled incoherently, and Rafe jerked his head, but neither opened his eyes. Frustrated, Spence grabbed each man by the hair and slapped his face back and forth. He got the response he desired. Both blinked their eyes and murmured.

Spence returned to his seat in the shadows next to the fireplace and waited. Slowly, Rafe opened his eyes, flashing them wildly about the room in front of him. Blood dripping from the corner of his mouth, he garbled his speech to the figure in the dark. "Who are ya?"

Spence remained silent, staring into the wild eyes of his prey. If his captive only knew who he was, there would be more than fear in his eyes; *there would be nightmarish horror*. And for good reason. He would soon have to realize what vengeance can do to a man, even a normal man—one not trained in the ways of killing. But to a man who had killed as many men as he had, a man who had faced death so many times—one who knows the art of inflicting pain and one who had all the reason in the world to even the score—then his victims *would truly be alarmed.* He decided to let them wonder about his identity. There was no rush in regard to that. Let them stew for awhile. They would find out when he was ready to tell them.

He had stayed awake many nights dreaming up the worst kind of torture for these two butchers. He had seen it all in Vietnam, and he, himself, had come close to begging to be put out of his misery. He had seen men go crazy, completely out of their heads, their tongues lapping out of their mouths like mad dogs, their eyes rolling uncontrolled in their sockets. And these men would be begging for mercy before he finished with them. *Some things in life were certain.* And he would relish every minute of their suffering before he would send them on their way to Hell—where he prayed they would be tortured for eternity.

"Why's he doing this?" Jake choked in a raspy voice, his eyes darting back and forth.

"Don't know. Must be crazy," Rafe said, spitting out blood and fragments of a tooth.

Spence continued to stare at his victims. He had waited a long time for this opportunity, and he planned to savor every moment of their fear.

"What are ya gonna do to us," Rafe snarled.

Spence moved out of the shadows toward the two men. "I'm gonna kill you. But I'm gonna take my time doing it. See this knife?" Spence drew a long sharp knife from its sheath. "I use this ta skin deer. I spect it will work just as well on vultures like you."

"You're crazy," Rafe cried, his eyes flashing wildly.

"No! *You're gonna be crazy.* Your mind will snap long before your body quits. I've seen it happen in Nam. I watched while they skinned some of my buddies. It's a helluva way to die." Vivid memories of the horrible scene he had just mentioned skipped through his mind. *The agony. The horror. The screams.*

"You'll never get away with it," Rafe growled.

"Maybe. Maybe not. But I don't give a damn, just as long as I get the job done." Spence pulled out another knife, wider and heavier than the first one. He stirred the coals in the fireplace till they emitted a red-hot glow, and then he buried the blade among them so that the handle remained off to one side. "Oh, yes," he continued, "once the skin has been pulled back, the exposed flesh is very, very sensitive— especially to hot metal."

Both men squirmed, trying to get loose but to no avail. The ropes were tied tightly around their wrists. The more they struggled, the deeper the ropes cut into their skin.

"You fucking maniac," Rafe screamed, as he nervously watched Spence, honing the long thin knife on a whetstone. "What did we ever do to you?"

"I don't like your mouth." Holding the blade and the stone in his left hand, Spence smashed his right fist into Rafe's face.

Rafe 's head jerked back from the impact. Blood spurted from his nostrils and mouth.

Spence thought of Marna suffering at this man's hand. "And, oh, yes! I think you deserve this too." He brutally kicked him in his testicles, smashing them.

"You dirty son-of-a-bitch," Jake sneered. "Cut us loose and we'll see how tough you are."

Rafe's sobs echoed throughout the cabin, as Spence approached the other man to shut him up too.

CHAPTER 22

▼

Joe had spent more time in the cafe than he had intended. After eating a steak sandwich, he had sat at the bar drinking one beer after another while pondering what he was going to say to Rafe. Maybe he shouldn't have come. Maybe it would have been better to stay in Winnipeg and just take off for the States when he had saved enough money. They had been his initial plans. What had made him change his mind? He wasn't quite sure. But one night on the job he had decided to confront Rafe face to face. And that's what he would do.

So immersed had he been in his thoughts, he failed to realize at first that the bar section was becoming crowded with local patrons. Soon, he too was caught up in the conversation, especially when some of the people discovered they had a Yank among them. They were more than curious *why* he was there. He had told them about his job in Winnipeg, and that he was driving to visit friends for the weekend. Happy they hadn't pushed for details, Joe had made his exit when he realized that he was starting to get lightheaded.

Walking toward his car, he checked his watch—11:35. It would be at least 1:00 a.m. before he reached Rafe's cabin.

When he finally turned onto the gravel road that led to his brother's place, he was getting more and more uptight. Burnt pine trees bordered either side of the narrow ribbon of road for miles. As the car zoomed along, its headlights illuminated the charred forest. The stillness and the blackness created an eerie atmosphere. After driving a tense five miles, Joe's nerves calmed a little when he could see where the rangers must have built their fire wall because charcoaled stubs blossomed into mature, healthy trees once again. Still he did not fully relax, knowing that no matter how much he had gone over the details of the impending conversation with Rafe, he would soon be on the receiving end of his brother's wrath.

As the road cut between two rocky cliffs, he knew that he was getting close to the turn off for Rafe's cabin. Slowing the car, Joe gripped the steering wheel trying to hold onto what little composure he had left. Sparks from a dangling hot wire dancing on the side of the road unnerved him.

*   *   *   *

Spence reached for the handle of the knife embedded in the coals. He pulled it from the fire and held it high enough so his victims could see the orange glow radiating from the edge of the hot metal. He had gagged both captives because he was annoyed by their agonizing screams, and he knew they'd get worse. He had thought he would enjoy their cowardly whimpering, but their torment affected him in an unanticipated way. He kept seeing the faces of his friends being tortured in Vietnam, mixed with those of the girls on the island, each time he approached the two squirming figures before him, their terrified eyes bulging.

Scenes of men tied to posts begging for mercy flashed through his mind. Their faces sweaty and shimmering from the reflection of the nighttime fires. Enemy soldiers laughed as they taunted and tortured their victims. Blood curdling screams echoed through the jungle. And then it would be light and he could see Marna struggling on the ground before him, her naked body bruised and bloody. The rigid figures of her friends dangling from ropes. He could hear their pleading cries to be spared. He could see the bloody knife of the butcher as he carved into flesh—hordes of flies covering their bodies.

And then the vultures swooped down among the carnage. They clawed at the open wounds till Spence held his hands over his ears, trying to block out his own screams.

The nightmarish visions slowly drifting from his mind, Spence wavered and then stumbled backwards into the cabin wall. He rested there, breathing heavily. For a time he didn't realize where he was. After coming to his senses and feeling the knife he gripped tightly in his hands, he staggered over to the fireplace.

Burying the blade once again in the bed of red-hot coals, he turned and faced the two wretches strung up before him. Disgusted with the feelings of weakness that racked his body, he forced himself to draw his skinning knife from its sheath. Determined to do what he had planned from that first moment he knew he had cheated death on the island, Spence slowly closed the gap separating him from Rafe. Rafe's eyes rolled wildly. They looked like two hot coals glowing in the dark. Rafe gurgled into his gag, blood backing up in his mouth choking him. His body convulsing spasmodically, a flood of urine flooded onto his legs and dripped onto the floor.

Nausea racking him, Spence reached out, grabbing Rafe's hair for support. With his other hand, he pressed the razor sharp blade to his victim's skin, blood trickling from a thin-lined gash. Sweat dripping from his forehead into his eyes, he gritted his teeth in a desperate attempt to rip the blade across Rafe's naked chest. But he couldn't make himself do it. *Again, visions of Marna writhing in agony filled his head. He could see her tortured face before him. Her screams pierced his skull. Blood oozing from her battered body, vultures plucking at her exposed flesh.* Howling in anguish, he stumbled backward, nearly falling into the open fire, his knife clattering on the floor.

"Goddamn you! Goddamn your souls to Hell," Spence wailed, holding his face in his hands.

*   *   *   *

Troubled by the severed electrical wire, Joe had parked his car a safe distance down the road and had walked up the lane toward the cabin. He was puzzled. There had been no storms in the area recently, and wires didn't break without a reason. *Had it been cut?* But why? He had carefully skirted the downed wire that continued to sizzle and dance alongside the pole. Nearing the porch, he had heard muffled screams coming from inside the house. Immediately he had conjured up horrifying thoughts that his brother and Jake were at it again—*torturing unsuspecting women they had picked up somewhere*. In disgust, he crept to a front window and peeked inside. His mind refused to accept the sight before him—Rafe and Jake stripped naked, dangling from the rafters. A man slouched against the wall by the fireplace. Easing the .45 from its holster under his jacket, he tiptoed to the door and nervously turned the knob as silently as he could. Slowly pushing the door open, he trained his eyes on the man who appeared to be sleeping, his back resting against the wall.

"Freeze!" Joe yelled, his voice quivering.

Spence stirred at the sudden intrusion, his mind still whirling from the terrifying flashbacks he had undergone. He struggled to stand up straight, his mind in a stupor, his body weak. Leaning back against the wall, he stayed put, trying to regain his senses.

"What the hell are you doing to these guys?" Joe shouted, his voice still a little shaky. "Don't move or I'll shoot."

His vision blurring, Spence tried to focus his eyes on the man with the gun. His insides begged to erupt, but he kept swallowing, forcing bile back into his stomach. Who was this intruder? How could he explain what he had been attempting to do to the men strung to the rafters. The man was young and not sure of himself. And that might make him even more dangerous with a loaded gun in his hand. Chances were he would never believe Spence's story. But why should he, coming upon such a scene? What was he doing here—unless maybe he belonged? *Unless he was Rafe's brother.*

Joe inched his way toward the stranger. "Stay where you are, or I'll kill you." Backing up toward Rafe, he kept the gun pointing at Spence's midsection. Glancing at his brother, he winced at the sight of his bloody face and his eyes rolling in their sockets. He pulled the gag away from his mouth, letting it dangle loosely about his neck.

"Rafe, can you hear me? Are you okay?"

His brother groaned, his eyes slowly settling down. Recognizing Joe, and seeing the gun in his hand, Rafe mumbled, "Shoot that fucker *now!*"

"No! Let me untie you and Jake, and then we'll figure out what to do with him."

"Well, goddamn it! Untie me. I'll shoot that crazy son-of-a-bitch!"

"I said 'no!' First, I'm gonna cut you loose, if you'll just cool it. Hey, you," he said to Spence, "kick that knife over here, easy like."

Spence eyed the knife for a second. He knew if Rafe and Jake were set free, it was all over. He would be dead. But what could he do? His sense of survival gradually overcame his nausea. Booting the knife, he sent it skittering over the floor toward Joe. He would have to act swiftly at his first opening. His body slowly coiling tight, ready to spring, he watched Joe bend over and pick up the knife. As Joe cut the rope above Rafe's head causing his body to collapse on him, he was forced to grab Rafe with both hands to keep him from falling to the floor.

Spence dove toward the fire and grabbed the end of a small burning log. Rolling off to the side toward the open door, he flung the sparkling log toward them.

Joe fired two wild shots that hit in the fire, scattering sparks all over the room. He then twisted in front of Rafe to ward off the firebrand hurling toward them. The blazing log hit the barrel of his gun and bounced onto the floor spraying sparks in every direction. The diversion had given Spence ample time to tumble through the open doorway.

After brushing hot sparks from his clothing, Joe looked toward Rafe slumped on the floor and then ran to the door. Nervously gripping the handle of his gun, he glanced outside to both sides of the doorway. No sign of him, so he kicked the door shut and bolted it. Then he backed toward Rafe and Jake, expecting the madman to come rushing into the cabin. He quickly glanced at all the windows. Still nothing. He grabbed the knife lying on the floor and cut away the rest of the ropes binding Rafe who had struggled over to the bed and flopped down. Then he freed Jake whom he helped to another bed. "Who was that fucker?" Joe asked.

"Don't know!" Rafe gasped. "He got the drop on us. He's plumb fuckin' crazy. Knew my name somehow."

"Well, I'm gonna get dressed and find that mother fucker." Jake rolled to the side of his bed and grabbed a pair of jeans from a dresser drawer. "Nobody fucks me over like that. Nobody!"

"We'd better wait till daylight. We'll never find him now," Joe said.

"Wait! *Bullshit!*" Jake yelled. "In the meantime, he's gonna come back for us like he did before. Let's get some flashlights and hunt that fucker down."

"I gotta stay here. He busted my balls real good. They're swelling up." Rafe lay on the bed, grimacing.

"All right. Stay put. We'll leave you my .38." Jake pulled on a sweatshirt over his head. "Keep your back to this wall and watch the door."

"Yeah! Yeah! Throw me some clothes and another blanket. I'm getting the chills." Rafe struggled to a sitting position. "You guys better stick close out there. He's a mean fucker."

"Where's the shotgun, Rafe?" Jake asked.

"Just off the porch somewheres. Less he took it."

Jake shined a flashlight toward the wall shelves between the two beds. Eyeing a box of shells, he grabbed at them, stuffing several into his pockets. "Got your flashlight, Joe? Let's get that crazy mother."

"Okay," Joe said, edging toward the door, but before opening it, he glanced toward his brother huddled on the bed, gun in hand. He hoped he would be safe there.

*   *   *   *

Spence had run from the porch around the side of the cabin where he had left his pack. He had grabbed it and disappeared into the darkness of the forest. After stumbling through the trees and bushes for several yards, he rested behind a pine and checked to see if he had been followed. When he realized that it was safe, he undid his pack and pulled out his .45 automatic, making sure it was ready. He cursed himself for allowing another slip up. He had blundered again and that bothered him. It was the delay that had done it. The delay in his decision to kill them. Delays like that would have cost him his life in Nam. He had been trained to kill quick and efficiently. No thoughts about taking a human life. Just do it. *Strange. He couldn't kill them when he had the chance.* And he had every reason to want to kill them. Somehow, he just couldn't do it. But now he might have to in order to save his own life. To save it for what? What had he to live for? There was that nagging thought again. Maybe nothing. But he had tracked those murderers down with a vengeance in his heart. That had been the only thing that had kept him going after the slaughter on Lake Alice. And finish this mission he would! *One way or the other.* He at least knew where they were. And they were probably wondering about him. He didn't know if they would have the guts to pursue him into the forest at night. After all, this was his playground. They were amateurs when it came to hunting a man down who could kill them at any minute they made a mistake. But had he not made a crucial mistake that let them kill Marna and the others? He vowed that this time they would not be so lucky.

Then he remembered the shotgun. He had known that it was lying in the grass near the cabin, but he didn't have time to pick it up. A scatter gun could make even a poor shooter dangerous at close range. He would just have to outwit them.

*   *   *   *

The cabin door opened, and two men appeared on the porch. They nervously flashed lights over the yard and surrounding timber. They seemed to be looking for more than him—probably the shotgun. They finally ventured into the woods in the opposite direction from where he hid. Spence waited till their lights all but disappeared into the dense forest, then he backtracked to the cabin. He wondered why the third man had not joined in the search. He hadn't figured on them separating, but that could be to his advantage, especially if he wanted to take them alive.

Pausing at the clearing before the cabin, he checked carefully to see if the two searchers had continued in their pursuit, or if they had decided to return. Feeling satisfied they were nowhere near to him, he crept toward the cabin staying in the shadows. He approached the side where he had picked up his pack. Peering in a window, he could see a man sitting up in bed staring toward the door. Light from the fireplace shone on Rafe's face. Why was he just sitting there? Knowing his temperament, Spence reasoned that he would have been the first to rush outside to try to catch up with him. But then Spence remembered how hard he had kicked Rafe in the groin. That must be it. *The man couldn't walk.* Whatever the reason, it was good knowing where he was.

Ducking back down, Spence headed behind the cabin toward the rabbit hutch. Slowly, he opened the door and grabbed one of the rabbits by the scruff of its neck. It squirmed, clawing the wood floor with its hind feet, but it didn't let out that blood curdling scream that rabbits in danger usually emit. The rabbit dangling comfortably in his grasp, Spence closed the hutch door and disappeared into the woods.

He hated killing the rabbit, especially when he did not intend to eat it, but he had plans that included the animal's blood. He knocked it on the back of its head with his pistol butt, killing it instantly. After stuffing it in his pack, he wended his way through the trees. He would circle around till he met up with the two who were searching for him. Spotting their flashlights off in the distance, Spence stopped. He placed the dead rabbit on the ground beside a tree where he could find it easily. Then he pulled a flashlight and long nylon cord from his pack. He methodically fastened the light to a branch of a thick bush. Then running the cord to the ground, he unraveled it to a point thirty feet away and tied it to a sapling. Returning to the flashlight, he flicked it on and then concealed himself behind a tree where he could hold onto the end of the cord without being seen. He gave it a few tugs which produced the desired effect he was aiming at. The light seemed as if it were being carried by someone walking through the woods. He hoped that his two adversaries would assume the same thing. He waited patiently, wondering how long they would search in the direction they were now heading.

*   *   *   *

Joe and Jake thrashed through the woods as fast as the darkness and terrain would allow. Flashing their lights in all directions, they kept a tight hold on their weapons—Jake with the shotgun and Joe his .45.

"Let's go back toward the cabin," Joe said. "I don't think he came this way."

"Never can tell. He's a sneaky son-of-a-bitch. He could be anywhere out here. But okay, we'll head back. It'll be light soon. We'll just stay at the cabin and wait for him to show himself."

After turning back toward the cabin, Jake nudged Joe when he saw the light bobbing in their direction. "It's him. Let's separate and take that bastard."

Both men, having turned off their flashlights, walked diagonally away from one another. Spence had been watching their movement. He thought what easy targets they made. They wouldn't have lasted long in Vietnam. They were the kind that had their throats ripped out on their first patrol. But nevertheless, he didn't want to underestimate them since they both had weapons—and one of them a shotgun. Even a random blast from a scatter gun could kill him, if the shooter was close enough and got lucky. And hadn't they gotten the drop on him back on the island?

He waited till they were twenty yards from the tree where he hid. If they got any closer, they would realize that he was not holding the light, shining in their direction.

"Stay where you are!" Spence called out. "You deserve to be killed, but I've decided to take you alive."

Both men froze in their tracks, eyeing the light in the distance.

"Why're you after us?" Jake edged toward the voice, his shotgun at the ready.

"You made a big mistake on that island in Lake Alice. You let me live." Spence cuffed his hands, shouting up into the trees, so as not to give up his hiding place.

Jake's thoughts flashed back to the bloody scenes that were still giving him nightmares. It couldn't be the soldier. He was dead when they left that island. He had to be dead. Rafe had shot him twice—once in the head even. But how could he know about that stuff unless.... *Unless he had been there?* He and Rafe had not told anybody else. In fact, they seldom talked about it even to one another. Maybe Joe had spilled his guts to somebody and that guy was after a reward or just wanted to be a hero. Yeah, that had to be it. He crept closer to the light. Whoever it was, he was going to blast him to pieces with both barrels at close range.

Joe had stayed put at the sound of the voice. There were not supposed to be any witnesses to their actions on that island. And that meant Jake and Rafe had killed all four of the girls and that friend of theirs. But then who was this guy? He watched as Jake slunk closer to the light. He himself moved off to the right of the beacon.

Within ten feet of the flickering light, Jake blasted away with both barrels from his shotgun. The glass from the flashlight shattered, leaving the woods in almost total darkness.

"I got the fucker," Jake yelled, hurrying as fast as he could toward the spot where the light had been. Reaching what he thought was the place, he flicked on his own flashlight and scoured the ground looking for the man's body. A severe crack on the back of his head sent him reeling into the bushes, unconscious.

Joe had trudged forward through the undergrowth at the sound of the shotgun blasts. He had trained his light toward the bushes in front of him, but he could see nothing.

"Jake, where are you?" He called.

A muffled voice said, "Over here."

"Did you get him?" Joe asked, moving in the direction of the sound.

"Yeah, I got him," Spence snarled, as he stepped from behind a tree and smashed his pistol butt onto the back of Joe's head. Joe wildly fired one shot, as he fell to his knees and then plunged headlong into the brush, completely out of his senses.

Spence wasted no time, as he tied their hands behind their backs. Then he took the dead rabbit from his pack and slit the animal's throat, causing warm blood to ooze from the wound. Rolling the two men over on their backs, he smeared the rabbit's blood all over their faces and necks. Turning on Joe's flashlight, he checked his work. Satisfied that his prisoners looked like they had been carved up by a butcher with a knife, he tossed the mangled rabbit aside.

In less than five minutes, Jake mumbled, twisting his head back and forth in the dirt. Spence immediately straddled him and gagged him. Then he poked Joe in the ribs and slapped his face a few times to speed up his recovery. When he started coughing, and Spence knew he was coming out of it, he tied a gag over his mouth too.

When they had both fully regained consciousness, Spence forced them to a standing position and shoved them toward the cabin.

"We're gonna pay Rafe a visit and cheer him up a little. By now he must be getting worried about you two," Spence said.

Both men, slobbering and gurgling incoherently, tried to catch a glimpse of their captor in the faint glow of morning light.

"Yeah, it's me all right. You left me for dead, and I damned near was. But I'm back. Just do as I say so I won't have to blow your brains out through your ears. Now get moving."

In their weakened condition, they had a difficult time making their way back to the cabin. But Spence kept herding them, driving them onward. When they fell, he yanked them to their feet and probed them in their backs with his gun barrel. The morning light slowly filled the woods, making it easier to at least see where they were going.

When they finally reached the clearing around the cabin, Spence halted his two prisoners in the cover of the trees. He eyed the cabin, looking for some sign of movement. Seeing none, he wondered if Rafe was still in the same position where he had last seen him. He knew he couldn't count on that for certain, and he didn't want any more slip-ups. He would have to end this madness and put them behind bars where they belonged. Caged like the animals they were. But first he would make Rafe taste fear like he had never known before.

As the morning mist engulfed the area, Spence shoved his two captives before him toward the cabin porch. Just in front of it, he pushed the two men on their faces to the ground. Then he rushed up on the porch as quickly as he could and looked in the window. He could see Rafe still on the bed, his eyes staring toward the door.

Returning to Joe and Jake who had struggled to their feet, attempting to get away, he forced them onto the cabin porch. When they had passed the window, he could hear Rafe screaming from inside.

"Who's there? Goddamn it!" And at that, Rafe fired two shots through the window.

"I've got Jake and your brother here. Don't you want to see how pretty they look? Don't shoot. I'll send 'em in." Kicking the door open, Spence shoved Jake sprawling toward Rafe.

Horrified, Rafe looked at the sight of the bloodied mess before him. "You fucker! I'm gonna kill you."

"You had your chance on that island. Remember, Rafe? But you're a piss-poor shot 'cuz I'm still alive."

Rafe's eyes widened. His mind reeled. *It couldn't be him. He was dead. He knew he was dead. He had to be dead.*

Jake struggled to get up and, in the process, tumbled onto the bed into Rafe. Rafe, frantically pushing his bloody face away from him, puked all over himself. Spitting and gagging, he stood up moving forward, firing his gun at the open doorway.

"Here's Joe!" Spence yelled from outside. Rafe paused to watch, as his wild-eyed and bloody-faced brother came flying at him.

Locked in an awkward embrace, they fell to the floor—the blood on Joe smearing Rafe's face and arms. Rafe tried to disengage himself. Rolling Joe away from him, Rafe fired at the open doorway till he emptied his gun. He was still pulling the trigger, making a click, click sound, as Spence stood above him and looked into his horror-filled eyes. If anything, Spence felt pity for his enemy, writhing on the floor like a mad dog. He had longed for this moment. Dreamed of getting vengeance since he had survived the island massacre. Anticipating the satisfaction it would give him kept him going. *But now he felt empty inside.*

The early morning sun, its light filtered by the trees, penetrated the cabin. He would drive these pathetic wretches into the nearest town and turn them over to the law. He hoped the fiendish nightmare was over.

About the Author

BIO

Allan Ede (rhymes with weed) was born in 1939 in Dubuque, Iowa. He attended a parochial grade school and a private military academy during high school. He received a B.A. and an M.A. in English from Loras College. He taught high school English, including creative writing, for thirty-six years and composition and literature at Northeastern Iowa Community College for four years. He coached basketball for six years on a freshman-sophomore level. He is the father of five daughters and one son.

Ede has had a variety of work experiences, including jobs in factories, construction, railroad, landscaping, painting, and selling Fuller Brush products from door to door in California. His hobbies include reading, writing, dancing, camping, and playing and watching most sports.

Ede has attended many writing conferences and workshops throughout the Midwest. He participated in a Novel Writing class, taught by a published author, for ten years.

Ede's credits include poems, articles, and short stories ("Fireflies" won 1st place in the Sinipee Writers' Short Story Contest). He has also co-authored *The History of Epworth, Iowa*. He has published *Rosalund's*

Raiders—a Young Adult novel about teen-age gangs. He is currently at work on his third novel.